USA TODAY BESTSELLING AUTHOR
Dale Mayer

TERK'S GUARDIANS
BOJAN 03

BOJAN: TERK'S GUARDIANS, BOOK 3
Beverly Dale Mayer
Valley Publishing Ltd.

ISBN-13: 978-1-773367-98-9
Print Edition

Books in This Series

Radar, Book 1

Legend, Book 2

Bojan, Book 3

Langdon, Book 4

About This Book

Haunted by a painful and unimaginable past, Bojan sought refuge in his work to keep the memories—and Lacy—at bay. But, when she raises the alarm over Bullard's family, Bojan is forced to step into the fray. Bullard is particularly wary of these "special" skills, except for those of Terk's team. Plus ignoring the offer of these skills can be dangerous—especially when a threat involves his family.

Lacy is helping the heavily pregnant Leia in the medical clinic, yet can't ignore the danger she sees. But triggering an alarm requires Terk's special brand of help, who then tags Bojan to step up and to handle it. Lacy had no idea Bojan would return to her in the near future. Maybe in some distant future? So finding him in the kitchen one morning is unexpected. Still, now is the time for assistance. She just doesn't know what help Bojan can offer. Or is *prepared* to offer …

Particularly as things go from bad to worse.

Sign up to be notified of all Dale's releases here!
https://geni.us/DaleNews

AS LEGEND AND Blair drove up to Guardian headquarters, she stared and gasped. "Oh my God, it really is a castle, isn't it?"

Legend laughed. "Not only a castle, it's a massive castle." He looked somewhat excited himself. "They're still trying to work their way through all the logistics of updating it."

She frowned at him and asked, "It does have indoor plumbing though, right?"

He grinned. "It does, indeed, have indoor plumbing. In fact, I understand the bathrooms have been massively updated and a few other things as well. ... So, some tolerance and patience will be required, but that will work both ways. We'll need to make a ton of adjustments, and so will they."

She nodded, as she got out. "It's so huge."

"It is, and they own acres and acres here, so lots of ground for you to explore. You can take Larry out for walks and all kinds of adventures." He grabbed his bags, and she grabbed hers, and they started for the front door.

Before they ever had a chance to reach for it, Larry came barreling out, with all the exuberance a ten-year-old could manage. He threw himself first into her arms and then into Legend's. "There you are," he screamed.

She laughed, the three of them in a three-way hug, as she

kissed Larry on the cheek. "Sounds like you're having a blast."

"Oh my gosh, it's amazing. Can we stay here? Can we stay?"

"Well, I'm not positive about that, but we'll see."

He looked up at her beseechingly. "Please, there's so much I can learn. You have no idea."

"Yeah, that's just because Clary is here."

"Well, that too," he agreed, with a big grin. He threw his arms around her neck and hugged her close. "I'm really happy that you guys are together too. It'll be almost like a real family."

"It *is* a real family," she stated. "No matter what it seemed like before, this is the real deal."

He looked from one to the other and got choked up. "You promise?"

"I promise," Legend vowed, wrapping an arm around her shoulders and then around Larry's. "Now, shall we go in and talk to the rest of the team?"

"Yeah, you don't even know who's all here," Larry added, "and you won't believe all the baby bumps." He looked at her and asked, "Have you got a baby in there yet?"

She flushed. "No, I hope not," she replied, embarrassed.

"Well, I wouldn't give it very long," Larry declared, "because you will be if you stay here."

"Why is that?"

As they walked inside behind him, they saw several of the women coming out of the kitchen with plates of food, only to stop and look at the newcomers. Blair saw the baby bumps, then she looked back at Legend. "What the hell?" she whispered.

"I have no idea," he muttered. He turned to Terkel, and

there stood Brody. "Funny how nobody mentioned that aspect," he said to Brody.

Brody laughed. "Well, we're trying to work on that aspect," he replied, "so we'll give you some pointers now that you're here. However, at the moment, you're the only couple who isn't in the family way." Then he stopped, chuckled, and asked, "Or are you?"

She glared at him. "I better not be."

He shrugged. "We all thought we weren't either, but it's apparently a hazard of this kind of energy."

"Okay, that's definitely a little disconcerting." Blair walked farther inside and was introduced to the group of people here. Some she knew of and some she didn't, but the first one to greet her was Clary.

Clary walked over, gave her a gentle hug, and said, "So glad to have you here. Larry has been an absolute treat to have around."

At that, Blair laughed. "And he tells me there's so much he can still learn that he definitely needs to stay."

"Well, it's a good thing you're staying then, isn't it?" Clary teased.

Blair smiled. "Well, at least for a while."

"Nope, no *at least for a while* nonsense," Terkel replied, as he assessed her with one quick clean look and nodded. "You'll do just fine."

She stared at him. "And you are?"

He grinned. "Terkel, grand master of this insane household."

She nodded. "Nice to meet you. I'm glad to know that you're an actual person and not just a voice in my head."

At that, everybody burst out laughing.

"Yeah," Terk confirmed. "I'm definitely a voice in your

head. I am also a real person, and we will all, at one time or another, be voices in your head."

Another woman walked up and added, "One of the first things we'll show you is how to get some privacy and peace and quiet around this place. In the meantime, we have an apartment for you."

Terkel, getting to business right away, stated, "We also have another job, although this one is a little different."

"Aren't they all?" somebody quipped. "I'm Gage, by the way," he told Legend and Blair. Gage sat down with a cup of coffee and asked Terk, "What's going on?"

"Bullard called. He has a woman who's apparently got some psychic ability, and, at the same time, he says that his wife is in trouble."

At that, another woman came up to Terk and wrapped her arms around him, saying, "In that case, you know what to do. We owe him ..."

Terkel nodded. "Yeah, I just have to come up with somebody to go help Bullard." Terk looked around at all the people gathered in the room.

"I'm not doing anything at the moment," said one man, leaning against the wall.

At that, Blair turned and recognized Riff. "You seem to be nowhere and everywhere," she said.

He nodded, giving her a lazy smile. "Yeah, that's me." Riff looked over at Terkel. "Bojan is already in Africa."

Terkel's gaze sharpened, and then he almost zoned out, right in front of them. Soon he nodded. "That would work perfectly," he said in a very soft whisper.

"You want to contact Bojan, or will I?" Riff asked.

"It'll have to be me," Terkel said, "but you might want to contact Bojan and tell him that I'll be calling."

"You think that'll make a bit of difference? He already knows."

"Yeah, he knows, but it might be easier if he knows that it's coming from you first."

At that, Riff laughed. "Okay, and what's the time frame on this deal for Bullard?"

"Well, how quickly can you get over there?"

"I can be there early in the morning, probably," Riff estimated. He glanced at Terkel and all the others. "Unless somebody else wants to go."

"No, this one's all about you," Terk noted.

"It won't be all about me. It'll be about Bojan," Riff stated.

"And Lacy," Terkel added.

At that, Riff's gaze narrowed. "Lacy?"

"Yeah, the psychic who's been warning Terkel," Gage confirmed.

"The university student in med school in Africa who has been working with Leia," Terk added.

Riff nodded. *"Lacy and Bojan."*

"Perfect," Terkel said. "Tell Bojan I want to talk with him, and soon."

And, with that, Riff nodded. "I'll go grab my bag."

CHAPTER 1

BOJAN ANTON LOOKED down at the phone ringing in his hand and winced. "Damn it, Terkel," he muttered to the empty air around him. "I don't want to talk to you." He just let it ring. When it rang a second time, he reluctantly went to answer it. This time it was a completely different number. He answered it with a smile on his face. "Hey, Riff. What's up?"

"Do you really think Terkel doesn't know when you're avoiding him?"

"Well, shit, it would really be nice if he wasn't in my face all the time."

At that, Riff laughed. "I'm not sure he knows any other way to be."

"Maybe not," Bojan admitted, "but I just came off a pretty shitty job, and I'm looking for some downtime. I'm not necessarily keen on running off to rescue somebody else right away."

"I hear you," Riff replied, "but I think you will want to deal with this one."

"Oh, I doubt it," he muttered, pinching the bridge of his nose. His energy was at an all-new low. "You guys, everybody in this business is always ready to jump right in, but … I'm totally okay to miss a few."

At that, Riff's tone turned sober. "Maybe, but this time

Lacy is involved."

Bojan sucked in his breath. His heart stopped for a long moment, before racing ahead, all signs of weariness dropping away instantly. "Well, shit."

"What's that?" Riff asked, with a chuckle. "Still want to sit this one out?"

"Back off," Bojan warned in exasperation, irritated, an almost instant reaction when Lacy came up in conversations.

Riff started to laugh. "God, I forgot what kind of a crazy relationship the two of you have."

"We don't have a relationship," Bojan snapped.

"On again, off again, on again and guess what? … Off again," he sang off key.

"Really?" Bojan glared at his phone. "You just called me to mock me?"

"Hey, if it works, hell yeah."

"You haven't explained what she's doing in this case. How is she involved, and how bad is it?"

"No, I haven't, and I'm not sure I should at this point," Riff acknowledged, with a snort. "As I recall, the last time you got into a mess with her, you threatened to send her to Timbuktu or someplace."

"I should have," he muttered. "Instead I just walked away." But, try as he might, he couldn't hide the odd note in his tone, and Riff heard it. Riff didn't miss much.

"Yeah? Well, guess what? This time you can get redemption."

"I'm not looking for redemption," he bit off, "and definitely not with her."

"Not a case of believing you or not," Riff stated, a smile evident in his tone, "because I can see some of the energy floating around the two of you, just as well as you can."

"You don't have to look," Bojan spat, again glaring at the phone. "It used to be that people stayed out of each other's way and definitely out of their faces."

"That's true enough, until we got into trouble anyway."

"Oh, yeah? You were more trouble than I expected you to be out there, so why would you even be trying to get other people into trouble?"

"Don't worry. I haven't lost sight of my goal either," Riff declared, sounding irritated, enough that it made Bojan smile.

"Yeah, and what about Angela?" Bojan asked. "I highly doubt she's giving you any rope, … unless it's enough to hang yourself."

"Well, she's still there unfortunately," Riff grumbled. "She's trying hard to get over to Terkel's place, but I don't think he has any idea how his life will change if she succeeds."

"Why the hell is she going to Terkel's?" Bojan asked, mildly interested. That made no sense.

At that, Riff paused. "I guess you don't know about all the changes in Terk's world, *huh*?"

Such a thread of mystery filled Riff's tone that Bojan perked up. "Don't know anything about it," he stated. "I deliberately went dark. Remember?"

"Yeah, I remember. I also remember it didn't do you much good, since we're all still calling you."

"And you can damn-well stop it," Bojan declared. "Do you not know the meaning of 'get lost'?"

"I do."

At that, Bojan hung up on his friend. Then he glared down at the phone because Riff hadn't told him what the hell Lacy had gotten involved in nor about the changes to

Terk's situation. Bojan groaned at that because, as much as he could try to convince himself that none of it mattered, it sure as hell did. It mattered a lot. But, worst of all, he knew that Riff would just sit there and would wait for Bojan to call back. Furious at having to give in, Bojan called Riff back. "Okay, all bullshit aside, what the hell is Lacy involved in?"

"Do you know Bullard?"

"Only by reputation," Bojan replied. "Why?"

"Somehow she managed to tell him that his wife's life is in danger."

"Wife? Bullard's married?" Shock filled Bojan's tone. "Did something happen to Levi?"

At that, Riff sighed. "Now see? Everybody knew about that aspect of Bullard's life, so why the hell we're keeping you out of the loop, I don't know."

"I'd rather be kept out of the loop completely than just get bits and pieces."

"To answer one question, Levi is fine, and he and Ice are still very happily married. Bullard found somebody for himself, after narrowly surviving an attempt on his life." Riff went on to share some of the details.

"Man, I didn't hear about any of that," Bojan admitted. "Sounds like he's damn lucky to be alive."

"The woman who rescued him saved him in other ways too," Riff added.

"Well, shit," Bojan muttered. "Seems I should get myself ditched on a deserted island, *huh*?"

"You and me both, buddy," Riff replied.

"No, you just need to stop running from Angela," Bojan suggested, with a laugh.

"I'm not running anywhere. That woman is a barracuda."

"No, she isn't. You just won't listen."

"I'm not listening. I'm doing everything I can to find whoever murdered her sister, and nobody wants that more than me, but I can't do what I can't do."

"I hear you on that," Bojan agreed, as he eased back on the teasing. "You still haven't explained what the hell Lacy is up to."

"I did tell you part of it. So, back to Bullard. Now that he's gone through so much, he is absolutely petrified of losing his wife, who is also pregnant, which was a huge shock for them."

"Damn," he said in amazement. "Who would have thought Bullard would ever get to that point?"

"Yeah, well, it's kind of like Levi and Ice—and, if you don't know what's happened to Terkel, that's a whole story in itself."

"Don't even start if you will try and tell me that Terkel has found a partner and is having a family," Bojan barked. "I just won't believe you, so don't waste your time." At that, Bojan started to laugh, but the lack of a response from Riff revealed something Bojan wasn't ready to comprehend. He stared down at the phone. "Shit, really?"

"Yeah, really, but that's not my story to tell, and it's just as bad, if not worse than Bullard's. However, at the end of the day, Terk also came out of it with a partner."

"Holy shit." At that, Bojan stared around at the empty hotel room he'd taken refuge in for the last few days, just to rest after his last job. "Is that what we have to do now to find someone special? We have to damn-near die?"

"Well, if that was all it took, we would both have partners already."

"Yeah, that's true enough." Bojan groaned. "So, what

the hell am I supposed to do with this information?"

"Bullard seems to think that Lacy is right. I'm pretty sure Bullard's contacted Terkel to check it out, and, as you already know, Lacy is somewhat accurate. She has a knack for sniffing out trouble."

"*Somewhat accurate* is right." Bojan snorted. "That also means, for the rest of the time, she's not accurate at all."

"Still, I wonder," Riff replied. "Anyway, the bottom line is that, because of her warning, Bullard—who has men all over the place, with teams everywhere—is shorthanded and is looking for extra help to keep his wife safe, plus to keep Lacy safe as well."

"What? Why keep Lacy safe?" Bojan asked in confusion, "I'm sure she dropped her bomb and blissfully set off into the middle of nowhere to do her thing again."

"You really do have a problem with her, don't you?"

"No, I don't have a problem with her. That would mean that I care, and I really don't give a damn."

"Then why did you call me back to find out what's going on with her?"

"Cut the games," Bojan snapped, his voice harsh. "Or the next time I hang up, that will be it."

"Well, you can," Riff replied. "Absolutely you can, especially if you don't want anything to do with this, but Terkel was trying to call you to see if you would go give Bullard some backup and help keep them safe while you're at it."

"I still don't understand what Lacy is doing."

"She's apparently attending university over there."

"University?" he repeated.

"Yeah, she's at med school over in Johannesburg."

"Med school, *huh*. Wow, the shocks just keep coming."

"You really haven't kept up with her, have you?"

"No, I haven't, and there are reasons for that. Remember?"

"Sure," Riff replied, "but she moved on with her life, and she is in med school and has been doing some practicum—work experience or something, I don't know—but with Bullard's wife, who is also a doctor."

"Well, shit," Bojan muttered, not knowing what else to say. "It still sounds highly unlikely that they need anything from us—or me."

"Yeah, it's definitely a *you* thing," Riff stated, "but I'm heading over to give a bit of assistance."

"What do you mean by that?"

"I'm more of a shadow these days," he said. "Sometimes that works for me, sometimes not, but I'll be in the background. I know that Bullard is over there, waiting for some help, and I won't let him down. He's always been there for me, and I know he's really shorthanded at the moment because a bunch of his guys are getting married or having families. It's like some sort of freaking pandemic," he muttered.

"Yeah, well, that wouldn't be Lacy though," Bojan added. "She can't have kids."

"I wanted to ask you about that. I thought I'd heard that."

"Yeah, it's true. I know she tried all kinds of tests, but it's just not to be," Bojan stated.

"*Hmm*, well, one of the tests that she has to do involves living at Terkel's place for a while," Riff shared. "That place is positively scary with burgeoning bellies at the moment," he muttered. "You can bet I was happy to take this job just to get the hell out of there."

"Burgeoning bellies? Terkel's partner too?"

"You have no freaking idea. Oh, and his whole team has gone private by the way."

"Private? Terkel?" Bojan felt like a parrot, and all he could do was repeat everything coming at him. "Jesus."

"Yeah, so I'll give you a few minutes to assimilate all this," Riff explained, "and then Terk will call you back. There is money in it, and I know for sure he's good for it. In fact, they're doing really well, but they're still trying to get set up."

"Where are they based?"

"England. In a castle of all things."

At that, Bojan started to laugh. "Good God, man. If anybody else had called me and had told me all this, I would have told them to call me back when they were sober and hung up, but I happen to know you don't drink."

"No, I don't drink, and, yes, it's a freaking castle. I saw it myself. That's where my gear is and where I'm staying these days, but, as I said, it was a good time to get out of there."

"Seriously, on the burgeoning bellies or whatever that was?"

"Every freaking one of them. It has something to do with the energy work, so, if Lacy is still unable to get pregnant, she needs to go spend some time with them because, I swear, it's contagious."

"Well, it's a good thing you and I aren't in that position then," Bojan muttered, shaking his head. "Whoever would have thought?"

"Nobody, that's the thing. Nobody would have thought, and this is all way too beyond me, but well—" Hearing noises in the background, Riff stopped. "That's my call for the plane. I've got to run. You've got a few minutes, and then Terkel will be calling you. Bye."

Bojan sat back on the hotel bed and looked around. It was kind of a sorry way to spend the last few days, as he had, but he'd just been so burned out and worn down from the last job that it had been this or go a bit stir-crazy. He'd done a private job for a friend, and, well, now he was footloose and fancy-free, but every time he was out for a few days, something came up, and he ended up back in the industry.

He never could quite break whatever connection kept him tied to that world. He had money, and lots of it, so that wasn't the issue. It had much more to do with trying to settle down and to find another way to make a living. Yet again it came back to the fact that he didn't need to make a living, but neither could he seem to walk away.

When his phone rang as expected, he glared down at it, then, finally giving in, he answered. "It's Bojan," he snapped. "What the hell is this all about? And did I hear that you will be a father?"

After a moment of silence on the other end, Terkel replied, sighing heavily. "You have no idea how my life has changed. On the other hand, if you would ever come for a visit, we could fill you in."

"Not when you dangle things about Lacy in front of me."

"Ah, it's still Lacy, isn't it?"

Bojan winced at that because, if there was ever anything to remember when dealing with Terkel, it's that you need to keep your damn walls up. Otherwise Terk would know everything there was to know about you. Bojan slammed his defenses up just then, but Terkel was already chuckling.

"A little too late, buddy, and, yes, she got herself into a bit of trouble, but I'm not sure it's trouble for her, as much as it's trouble for the rest of us."

"Meaning, Bullard."

"We are one," Terk declared. "If Bullard needs us, we're there. He helped us out, and we'll help him out."

"Of course there's always Levi and his team."

"Levi will always be part of the family too," Terk stated. "No way he can't be."

"That's because you and Merk are family," Bojan noted in exasperation, "but that's got nothing to do with me."

"Except for Lacy, and she's definitely got something to do with you."

"What's the job?" Bojan asked abruptly, just to adjust Terk's focus.

"Go give Bullard a hand."

Bojan frowned at that. "But there are strings with the job, is that it?"

"No, not so much strings. You would just be hired muscle," Terkel replied calmly. "However, considering that Lacy made this observation, and we know that your energy and Lacy's energy are much stronger together, it would be very helpful if you could confirm or deny what's going on in Bullard's world."

"Why me? You could do that yourself."

"I get that something is drawing in Lacy's energy," he explained, "so that's one of the reasons I'm pulling some strings to try and get people over there to help. And, if need be, I'll go over there because I won't leave Bullard in his time of need."

"And yet you also have a pregnant wife, according to Riff," Bojan noted. "Believe me. I'm still adjusting to that idea."

"Don't get me wrong. I will go if need be. The struggle isn't that it's right or wrong. The struggle is just trying to adapt to how my life has changed. I have people here I can leave Celia with. I simply won't desert Bullard, not after he's come to our rescue so many times.

"No, of course not." Bojan sighed. "Fine. But if Lacy gets in my head again—"

"She will get in your head because she already lives in your heart," Terkel declared, his voice calm, "and, if you think I'll pull any punches about that, you're wrong."

Bojan glared at the phone. "I really, really hate it when I'm around people who know more than me."

"The only reason you hate it is because you're still resisting. You also know that your abilities, which you continue to deny, are much stronger when you're close to Lacy."

"Yeah, and I don't understand that." Bojan moaned. "I've tried to use these so-called abilities you keep talking about *without* her, and they don't work."

"That's because you're a matched set," Terkel stated. "And, like a lot of matched sets, you don't function quite so well on your own."

"Yet she appears to be functioning just fine," he pointed out.

"No, I don't think so, and I think that's why she's only getting a partial reading. She can't get any more information on it."

"That doesn't mean I will either."

"No, and I have a fair bit of information, but we don't have any idea who or when."

"Which means you haven't got anything," Bojan muttered in disgust. "And what about Riff?"

"Riff's headed over already. He's on a plane, or he should be." After a moment's pause on the phone, Terk added, "Yeah, he's on the plane now," which matched up with what Riff had told Bojan.

"And?"

"You're a whole lot closer, and you could be over there yourself fairly quickly."

"I could." He hesitated. "So, Riff told me that you guys have gone private, *huh*?"

"Yes, and that's another viable point that I still haven't gotten used to bringing up. We're no longer a part of the CIA or any government body, although we are taking contracts from all of them," he shared, with a note of humor. "I'm quite happy to take money from them, if it comes to that, but, in this case, we'll be paying your wages."

"I don't come cheap," Bojan pointed out.

"I know you don't, and, although this isn't what I would consider a high risk job, because of who needs us and what the issue is, obviously I'll be paying top dollar."

Bojan frowned at that. "When you put it that way, it somehow makes me feel like a sleaze."

And Terkel burst out laughing. "Okay, well, anytime you want to give me a discount, feel free. The bottom line is, I need help, and either you're there or you're not. I just need to know."

"Fine, I'm there," Bojan groused. "I'll get there in my own time though."

"Of course you will." Terk laughed. "I'll tell Bullard, but I won't tell Lacy. How's that?"

"Knowing her, she already knows anyway," he muttered.

"It could be the time for you two to settle your differences."

"Not likely," he muttered, as he went to disconnect the call. "Some things are just unforgivable."

"No, they aren't," Terkel argued. "They just take a little

more time and understanding, and it really helps if you get the full story."

And, with that, it was Terkel who ended the call.

LACY MARRIOT HAD been busily working in the surgery suite, tired from an already long day. She stretched, and, when her arms dropped, a thought slammed into her brain. It was so strong, so harsh that she stumbled back a step. Bullard turned toward her and frowned. She gave a headshake. "I'm fine," she murmured. He just raised an eyebrow and continued to stare. She winced. "Bojan is here."

His lips twitched. "Wow. Have you got an antenna for him or something?"

"Yeah, maybe," she muttered, glaring at him. "Not one I particularly appreciate."

"Life is like that," he replied, with a nod. "And considering the weird *knowings* you've got going on here, I'm not at all surprised that Terkel suggested that Bojan come over."

"Of course he suggested it," she muttered caustically, "but I'm surprised Bojan actually answered the call."

Bullard shrugged. "Terkel can be pretty persuasive."

"Maybe, ... it still surprises me though. The very fact that I'm here would typically be enough to keep Bojan away."

"Not this time." Bullard gazed at her sharply, shaking his head at their dynamics. "Will you be all right?"

"Of course," she snapped, glaring at him. "It's not as if I haven't seen him time and time again."

"No, but still, this time could be different."

She shrugged. "Doesn't matter. He's already here." At

that, Bullard turned and looked around the room, then back at her. She understood the confusion in his expression. "He's out in the kitchen, probably having coffee, or at least he will be in the next ten minutes."

Bullard's eyebrows shot up, and he turned and walked out of the surgery suite, leaving her alone.

Which was a damn good thing because just knowing that Bojan was here didn't mean she was ready to deal with him. She'd had a pretty strong suspicion that he was on his way but hadn't allowed herself to analyze the information that had been racing toward her. She'd always had an early alarm system where he was concerned, but then, when you love somebody as much as she loved him, you just couldn't catch a break. No matter what he said or did, she was as susceptible to him as ever, and it just pissed her off.

Finally she finished cleaning up the surgery suite, and, stripping off her latex gloves, she threw them into the garbage bin and stepped out of the room. She was tired, fed-up, and the last thing she wanted to deal with was Bojan right now. She walked into the kitchen, knowing there was really no way to get out of it. Better to face the devil you knew right up front, and, as she walked in, the familiar drawl hit her.

"There she is," Bojan greeted her, calmly looking over at her. "What kind of trouble did you get me into now?"

"I didn't get you into any trouble," she stated calmly, as she walked to the coffeepot. Multiple people were around—some she knew, and some she didn't—but that was just how it went around here. She poured a cup of coffee, then rubbed her temples. The headache that had started earlier was now at a massive crescendo. When Leia looked over at Lacy in concern, Lacy smiled. "I'm fine. You've got enough on your plate to worry about, so no need to add more to it."

"That doesn't mean I'm not concerned when a friend is dealing with a headache that just won't go away."

"Yeah, well, it just got compounded." Lacy shot Bojan a hard look.

He gave her a benevolent smile. "Right back at you, honey."

She looked over at Leia. "You really had to call him, *huh*?"

"Bullard felt we needed some extra help," she explained. "I told him it would be fine, but he didn't want to take any chances. Terk agreed."

Lacy muttered, "Bullard won't take any chances, particularly given your current situation."

"Oh, thanks," Leia said, followed by a giggling laugh. "Sure, go ahead. Remind everybody that I'm built like a whiskey barrel."

"A whiskey barrel?" Bullard repeated, as he walked over and bent down to give her a gentle hug. "That is hardly how I would have described you."

"Well, it's how I feel," she muttered. "A whiskey barrel with stick legs."

Lacy had to grin. "Still, you're the prettiest whiskey barrel I've ever seen."

At that, Leia rolled her eyes. "If that was meant to help, well, thank you, I think."

"Yeah, that probably didn't help, sorry." She stared down at the coffee which was hot but kind of tasteless. "I'm really tired, so, if you'll excuse me, I'll go get some rest before dinner." With that, she turned and walked out of the kitchen. She knew Bojan couldn't resist tormenting her, and, sure enough, he called out behind her.

"What's the matter? You running away already?"

"No, I'm not," she declared, "but I'm tired, fed-up, and the last thing I need right now is anything to add to my headache. If you're still around, maybe I'll talk to you in the morning, but I need a nap right now."

She knew she had surprised him, but she'd changed. At least she hoped she'd changed. This was one of those tests where she would see whether she really had changed or if she would slide back into the same damn pattern she'd been trying so hard to get rid of. She voted for change, but it seemed as if her body didn't give a crap what she wanted. The fact that Bojan didn't want her and that she still wanted nobody else was a cross to bear that she couldn't seem to find any way around. She understood why, to some degree, but he was wrong, and he didn't want to listen to reason. So it just didn't matter.

Up in her room, she closed the door, sank onto her bed, and let the hot tears flow. Every time she saw him, the tears came. It was as if she had no way of hiding her feelings, and that drove her to madness. He was a hell of a man. She was a hell of a woman. It seemed they were two sides of the same coin and yet were never meant to join up. Although they had once, and that was part and parcel of the problem.

She sagged back on her bed, grabbed the loose blanket that she kept on the side, then rolled over and closed her eyes. Thankfully sleep came quickly.

CHAPTER 2

WHEN LACY OPENED her eyes not too much later, she felt a little sense of peace. Bojan was here, and she would deal with it, just as she always did. Nothing would ever make her life easier when it came to Bojan. It was what it was, and it was something she must deal with. She got up, and, stepping under a hot shower, she let the water cool down at the end, to wake her up and to fortify her for what was to come. As she stepped out and quickly dressed in a light dress and sandals, she made her way back downstairs, ready for dinner.

Most of the team seemed to be in the dining room, seated around that huge table. However, a smaller group still sat at the kitchen table. Lacy walked over to Leia and asked, "Did you get a nap?"

She looked up at her, shook her head. "No, of course not." As she stood up, she winced.

Immediately Bullard was there to help her. "Is it time?"

"No, it's not time," she replied crossly. "Unless you're trying to ask if it's time to go lie down before dinner. Because, for that, it is time."

At that, Bullard called out to the others, "I'll be back in a few minutes." Then he quickly escorted Leia from the room.

Lacy walked over to put on the teakettle, then she poured herself a glass of lemonade from the fridge.

"Still drinking tea, I see," Bojan noted.

"Tea, coffee, whatever," she muttered. "I don't mind which. Some things are just really not that important, but right now lemonade hits the spot when it's hot out."

"Did you get some sleep?" Bojan asked in concern. "That headache seems to be getting worse, *huh*?"

"It'll ease up soon," she noted, with a weak smile. Still holding the pitcher of lemonade, she turned and looked at the others. "Anybody else?"

Ryland hopped up. "That's a damn good idea."

"I figured you would be into the beer by now," Lacy teased.

"Yeah, I probably should be, but I'm just as hot and as tired as the rest of you right now."

She added, "You just came back from a job, so you must be due for a break."

"A break is one thing, but, as you well know, around this place, we're just as likely to end up going right back out again."

"Sometimes," Lacy agreed, "but, hey, as long as Leia's okay."

They all walked into the nearby dining room to join the others there.

"Do you guys know anything about what's going on?" Ryland asked. "I just got in, so I haven't caught up."

At that, Bojan laughed and shook his head. "We better ask Lacy here for those kinds of answers. Apparently she's the one who sounded that alarm."

She groaned at that. "Well, I didn't do it on purpose," she muttered, as she stared around the massive dining room table. The kitchen was off to the side and behind them, but multiple coolers were kept out here with drinks for all the staff, which appeared to number close to twenty at any given time. She looked over at Ryland. "I thought you were off on a job that was expected to last some time?"

"Yeah, I was, but we're done early."

"So, in that case, you don't need extra staff here to help look after Leia, do you?"

Ryland frowned. "We already have two other jobs lined up. I'm leaving soon for one, and Eton's leaving in the morning for the other." He added, "Nobody mentioned anything about Leia being in trouble, so why don't you fill us in?"

Lacy winced at that. "I think that's for Bullard to do."

At that, Bullard returned to the room, and, hearing the last bit of conversation, he shook his head. "No, that's definitely something for you to do."

She groaned. "Look. Every once in a while, I get … visions," she admitted. "That's all I can really say, and I had one that forewarned Leia was in trouble." Ryland, Eton, and Cain sat there quietly, though she wasn't even sure when Cain had joined them, not until she sat down. Unfortunately she was the center of attention, with Bojan looking at her a little too closely for her taste.

"Visions?" Cain repeated.

She glared at him. "I get it. You guys don't really know me, and that's fine, but, for background or maybe just to make me sound like I'm not quite as flaky as you're thinking, you might want to contact Terkel."

At that, all three men's expressions cleared, and, sitting back, they glanced at each other.

Ryland spoke first. "So, Terk knows?"

She nodded. "Terkel knows and agrees."

At that announcement, a whistle rippled across the

room, as the men now looked at her with respect. "Are you part of his group?"

"No, I'm not, although he's brought it up a couple times," she admitted. "I'm just not there yet." As it was, the intensity of their gazes got to be too much, and finally she raised both hands in frustration. "That's it. I'm not going there. I'm not explaining anything more. I just can't, so all of you can just turn your attention elsewhere."

As one they all turned to Bullard, who gave them a wolfish grin. "I knew that you would all want to stay in town, but we also have jobs that we've had lined up for quite a while, so I need you guys to get out there and to do this."

"So you brought in extra people to look after one of our own?" Cain asked, his voice rough. He was clearly hurt.

Bullard frowned at him. "I wouldn't have, but we've got commitments, and you lined up these jobs yourself, as I recall."

"Sure I did, but I would certainly get someone else to cover it, if needed."

"But that's just the thing, it's not needed," Bullard asserted. "And believe me. Leia knows of the threat, and she seems to think we're making too much of it as it is."

Eton shook his head. "If Terkel says it's an issue, then it's an issue," he declared, his voice curt and dry. He turned to look at Lacy. "No offense intended."

"None taken." She shrugged. "Terkel's got the rep. I don't. I went to Bullard. Bullard went to Terkel. Terkel agrees with me, so we're all good," she replied. "Now, if Terk didn't agree, I don't know what I would have done," she admitted, with a grimace, "but thankfully it didn't come to that."

"If Terk agrees with you, that's good enough for me,"

Eton stated.

"Thank you for that," Lacy muttered. "Not everybody has the same belief system."

"We've been in some pretty rough situations, and Terkel has bailed us out, more than a few times," Eton shared, his voice sincere. "If something's going on with Leia"—he turned to glare at Bullard—"we all want in on it."

"I know that," Bullard snapped, glaring back at all of them. "But we also have a business to run, and we can't do it all without contractors coming in to play as well. Some of these clients have requested specific people for very particular issues, and you've all agreed to these jobs, so I won't pull you off. I figured it would be better to have you guys get out there and knock out those jobs while you can and then get back home."

At that, the three men looked at each other for a moment, until Ryland shrugged. "Fair enough." Cain muttered something similar. Eton still glared at Bullard.

At that, Dave walked in with a stack of files that he dropped in front of Bullard. "Seeing as she's gone down for a nap ..."

Bullard looked at him and sighed. "Meaning?"

"Meaning. these are all potential cases, people, and entities that could be after her."

"Why would they be after Leia?" Bojan asked. "Does she have some sort of history in our work?"

"No, but she's been a doctor for years," Bullard noted absentmindedly. "We recently closed a big case, involving a surgeon killing his own patients on the operating table. Leia caught him at it years earlier but had no way to prove it, and he ended up destroying her life and career. She had material stashed away on him that finally took him down in the end, but, by doing that, it's entirely possible that we may have stirred up something else."

"*Great*," Bojan muttered, frowning at Bullard. "You just instinctively know how to attract trouble, don't you?"

At that, Bullard gave him a ferocious grin. "Yeah, but I also know how to fix it," he declared. "Believe me. If somebody makes a move on my place, they won't walk away. I'm not leaving enemies behind to come and terrorize us down the road," he stated flatly. "If you've got a problem with that, you can go back to Terkel right now."

"I don't play fetch or carry well at all, and I sure as hell don't go back to Terkel for anything," Bojan snapped, glaring at Bullard. "If you're looking for a puppy dog to train, the answer is hell no."

At that, Bullard burst out laughing. "I've never known anybody around Terkel's circle to be trainable," he shared, still chuckling over the idea. "But, if he sent you, I know you can do the job, and I'm all over the need for extra help because, right now, regardless of how my team here is feeling about it, we need another pair of eyes to stay close to Leia and Lacy."

"Why Lacy?" Bojan asked.

At that, Lacy snorted. Ignoring her reaction, Bullard calmly responded, "Because you'll pick up further clues that way."

"How so?" Bojan questioned.

"She's the one who picked up on the danger that we're facing now, and I don't want to lose out on Lacy's early alarm system because somebody decides it will cramp their style."

At that remark, Lacy felt Bojan's gaze switch to her, but she refused to look at him. He didn't say anything more, but neither did he back down, and she knew it was definitely not a done deal. She sighed. "For those of you who don't know, Bojan and I have some history," she shared, with a wave of her hand. "Old ancient history which I was kind of hoping he would get over, but he hasn't. Since I consider it his problem, I'm not dealing with it. … On that note, you guys can go do whatever. I'm off. I'm done, and I'm tired. I'll go grab some food, then I'm hitting the pool."

Then she got up and walked out, leaving them to stare, first at her back and then at Bojan.

AFTER LACY'S MAJESTIC exit, it was all Bojan could do to *not* burst out in applause. He raised one eyebrow and stared at the rest of the men. Bullard looked at Bojan and asked, "Will it be a problem?"

"Not for me," he replied. "I just need to know the parameters of the job."

Bullard turned and stared at the new man full-on. "The parameters of the job are to look after them, both of them," he declared, his voice harsh, "regardless of your feelings." When Bojan remained silent, Bullard nodded. "Good, then there's no problem."

But Bojan could tell Bullard wasn't satisfied with that. So Bojan knew the topic would be coming up again later.

Just then Dave spoke up. "With that out of the way, maybe we can take some time now to go through some of these files."

"I'll have a look," Bojan stated, as he held out his hands.

At that, Dave handed off several files to him, while the other men mumbled, yet reached for files as well. With the files divvied up, Bojan quickly went through some of the summaries on top of each file and noted they involved court cases to do with the surgeon Leia had taken down and the hospital that had lawsuits against him. The third one down caught his interest.

He stopped and looked at it, tapping his finger. He knew, on an energy level, this one needed a closer look. He raised his gaze and gave a quick glance at the rest of the files, but not one of them gave him so much as a buzz. He pulled this one out of the stack, opened it up, then, using his finger to speed-read, as he'd learned decades ago, he quickly went through the entire file. Then he plopped down the file, got up, and poured himself some lemonade. He returned to the table and sat, pushing away the other files, and just stared at the glass. The speed-read had worn him down, but he still felt good.

After a few minutes of awkward silence, somebody cleared his throat and asked, "Bojan?"

He raised his gaze and stared. "What?"

Eton pointed at all the files. "You only looked through that one file and didn't even open most of the others. Yet you seem to be done. Why?"

"It's this one," Bojan declared, tapping the file.

Everybody froze, staring at him, then at the file.

Bullard sighed. "How do you know?"

Bojan threw back the rest of the lemonade and set the glass on the table. "The same way Lacy knew there was trouble," he stated flatly. When everyone's gaze focused on him, he added, "If that's a problem, you better check in with Terkel."

With that, he headed to the kitchen. Immediately came a buzz behind him, as he assumed that Bullard would reach for his phone. When Bojan heard Terkel's name mentioned, he smiled and stepped outside—and froze at the sight of a mermaid in a teal-blue bikini floating in the pool. Just resting, as if she'd been through an arduous day. Then he remembered what Terkel had said about her training to be a doctor.

He didn't know what specialty she was in, but he could imagine. For his part in that, he was sorry, but he'd never been able to tell her. They could never be in the same room and talk for more than five minutes without one of them getting up and walking out in anger and frustration.

He knew perfectly well what the problem was, but he still wasn't ready to settle down, and, even if he were, he wasn't at all sure he was ready to settle down with somebody who could read both his mind and the thoughts in his heart as easily as she did. Surely a man was entitled to some privacy. Yet, when the two of them were around each other, it was like two locomotives banging up against each other, until finally the one managed to push back the other.

So far it was usually him, but he suspected she had gotten stronger in many ways because the woman in front of him right now was cool and composed, and her energy was in much better control than his own.

Swearing softly, he turned and stepped back into the kitchen, only to find Bullard standing there, his hands on his hips, glaring at him.

"What?" Bojan barked, glaring right back.

"You want to come and explain yourself?" Bullard snapped, his voice tight. "I get that your mind is on that woman out there, but my mind is on my very pregnant wife and the danger to her."

Bojan followed Bullard into the dining room, where the

rest of the men sat and waited.

Eton spoke first. "Can we get an explanation of just what's going on here?"

Bojan turned to him. "Terkel called and asked if I would come and help out because he owed Bullard."

"Got that, but why you?"

"I'm an independent agent. Terkel has been after me for a long time, and he also knows about Lacy."

"What about Lacy?"

"That she has gifts. And, as she already put it so plainly, we have a history, so let's leave it at that," he replied coolly. "I don't wish her any ill will, and I'll certainly protect her while she's here. As far as the rest, I read *energy*, … for lack of a better word. It's this intuition that Lacy and I have, and it usually points me in the right direction on something. Lacy's energy and mine work better together, or so Terk has led us to believe. As to all these cases, if anything is a threat within that stack, it's coming from that file. And, if it doesn't have anything to do with Leia or Lacy, then that's another problem right there."

Eton sat back, looked over at Dave, and stated, "Well, there you go, Dave. It's all solved."

Dave just sighed. "Haven't you figured out yet that, when somebody like Terkel gets their hands on this shit, all hell breaks loose," he pointed out.

"Yeah," Eton agreed. "We end up getting to the bottom of the problem and generally fast, but it's usually bloody, and it's hard, and it's intense, with no holds barred because whoever is up against somebody like Terkel is generally bad news for the rest of us."

At that, Bojan looked over at him, chuckling. "I gather you know Terkel."

Eton's expression suddenly changed, when an affectionate smile appeared. "Absolutely. The man is gold, and he's never steered us wrong, but his cases tend to be convoluted, twisted, and not the easiest to solve. That's why, when Terkel says *jump*, I jump. Yet, at the same time, I know that, when I land, I'll still be damn confused. So you've given us about 10 percent of what we need to know. Want to fill in the rest?"

"I can't give you anything else. My *energy* doesn't work that way for me. All I can tell you is, … this case is important." He turned to tap the file, only to realize that Eton had already taken it and was going through it.

"So, ten years ago a woman with cancer died on the table, and the death was attributed to the same doctor," Eton muttered.

"Right, so what's your problem with that file?" Bojan asked.

"The problem is, … what does that death a decade ago have to do with the here and now?" Eton frowned at Bojan. "How can we know for sure?"

"What I can tell you is this," Bojan explained. "If that case isn't connected to Leia, it's still a problem in itself today."

"And why?"

"Because he was paid to do it."

"Paid to do what?"

"That case, that patient, the doctor was paid to kill her, and he did. However, somebody else got off scot-free and is pissed off that his murdering machine is no longer available, since he has somebody else he needs knocked off."

Ryland sat back and let out a low whistle. "*Huh.* That would hamper somebody's style, and I can see why they would be pissed off at Leia, considering she was responsible for putting away the doctor."

"Exactly," Bojan confirmed. "That's not necessarily the whole answer. However, you haven't given me more information, so I can't tell you whether any of the other information is right or wrong."

"Is that what you are, a lie detector?" Eton asked curiously. "Because, man, we could sure use somebody like that around here."

"No, not a lie detector," Bojan corrected, "but I can generally see positive and negative energy. And, no, that doesn't always work either because that would be way-too-fucking easy," he snapped. "Sometimes I mess up big-time."

At that, the men stared at him for a long moment, then looked past him to the pool.

He nodded. "So, if you don't mind, that conversation is over."

"Got it," Bullard noted, but his lips twitched. "You might find that being here is good for you too."

"I'm not so sure about that," he argued. "Just because it's history, that doesn't mean it's a good history."

CHAPTER 3

LACY WOKE THE next morning with a smile on her face but then groaned, as memories of the previous day slammed into her. She'd had a hard time sleeping, until she finally did a series of meditations, guaranteed to remove some of that disturbing energy in her system, and finally she'd crashed. Now, as she rolled over and checked the clock, she realized it was already late.

Just before she hauled herself out of bed, she remembered it wasn't a surgery day here at Bullard's main African compound, which housed a huge free clinic for the public. It was Saturday, so technically she had the day off. Not that there was very much in the way of time off here because, when other people were in need, Bullard's team all stepped up and got to work. But, in Leia's case, she was working too much, and they needed to dial back down her surgical hours again.

To start her day off, Lacy put on a bathing suit, slipped on a cover-up, grabbed her towel, and headed to the pool. She was surprised to find it empty, and, quickly throwing her things aside, she dove in and set about doing her laps. When she finally stopped and came to the shallow end, panting, Dave stood there, waiting.

He had a huge grin on his face and a smoothie in his hand. As he held it out for her, he said, "This one's special. I doubled up on the protein and added some oils to help calm your nerves."

She rolled her eyes at him. "*Right*. Any particular reason for the nerve tonic?"

He gave her a big fat smile. "Not at all," he muttered, "but sometimes life tosses us curve balls, and we don't always appreciate it, so knock it out of the park."

She winced. "I guess everybody is wondering what's going on, *huh*?"

"No, I think they all know exactly what's going on," he replied, "just not the details."

"Well, at least Bojan said something," she muttered. She took a sip and stared up at Dave. "You forgot the apple juice."

"I didn't want to give you anything too sweet," he explained. "You've been having blood sugar rushes lately."

She sighed. "This tastes like …" Then she frowned.

"Like what?" Dave asked.

"Dried hay, rolled out in the mud, and left to ferment."

He burst out laughing. "I know it's not that bad."

"Are you sure about that?" she asked. "Maybe you're not thinking it through."

"Oh, I'm pretty sure I'm thinking it through," he argued, with that big smile. "Bottoms up."

"I suppose you made one of these for Leia too."

"Yes, but hers is a little different. She needs extra vitamins."

"Makes sense, considering she's extremely pregnant."

There. She'd said the word. It was something that she avoided saying as much as she could. Turning her back on Dave, Lacy walked over and sank down on one of the lounge chairs, feeling the chill set in already. She never understood how she could be cold after a workout, but she still managed to find chills, even here in sunny Africa. When that hit her, the others generally looked at her in surprise, but it all depended on how much energy she had burned through during the exercise.

"Breakfast will be ready soon too," Dave shared cheerfully.

She looked over at him. "I can just come in and get something easy. I'm running late."

"Yeah, you are, but everybody is today. They stayed up talking pretty late themselves."

"Good," she muttered and then yawned.

"It seems you didn't get anywhere near enough sleep."

She shrugged. "I got enough."

"Considering today is not a surgery day, maybe you should use the opportunity to take care of yourself too. You can't keep burning the candle on both ends."

She gave him a flat look. "Why not? I've been doing it for a long time."

"There's a cost that rolls around for that too," he warned her, "and you're about to hit it." With that, he turned and walked away.

She could do nothing but groan behind him. Everybody here was always so concerned about keeping her comfortable, yet what was really hard to adjust to was how many people knew her business, knew what was going on. That would be one of the biggest problems with having Bojan here.

People would be curious, questions would be asked, and issues would be raised. Right now, she would do her best to lock them all out, but it wouldn't work when they were on top of each other. Particularly not when Bojan did energy work that made him very skilled. Whether Bullard's team knew it yet or not, they were lucky to have Bojan. Considering that he would be assigned to her, Lacy knew perfectly well that she was lucky too. She didn't want to be lucky, at least not in the way it was happening right now.

Shaking her head, she downed the rest of the shake and waited for her stomach to settle. As much as she knew the smoothies were good for her, they didn't always settle as easily as they should. Some of it was nerves, and some of it was just pouring too much *goodness* into an already touchy stomach.

Once her stomach calmed down enough, and she felt herself warming up, she threw on her coverup to help protect against the bright sun, then got up and headed into the kitchen. She sniffed the air as she walked in. They had full-time chefs now because, with so many of them, Dave couldn't handle it all, plus his other duties. Besides, Dave had a wife now himself, and she was one of the catering chefs. Therefore, she had hired somebody else she had known for many years to help as well.

Lacy sniffed the air again and murmured, "It smells lovely in here."

At that, Pia turned and gave her a big grin. "You're too skinny. My breakfast will fix that."

"Great, so it takes just the one meal, and I'll be totally okay, right?" she teased, with a laugh.

"No," he snapped, "but you stay here longer, and, sure enough, we'll get some weight on you."

"I don't need weight on me," she argued, with an eye roll.

He looked at her and repeated, "You're too skinny."

"Thank you for that," she quipped in exasperation, "but I hardly think that's the case." He just shrugged. "Fine, when is breakfast?"

"I'm just bringing it out, so you go sit. Everybody is already there."

"I'll go get changed first then." Not giving him a chance to argue, she headed upstairs, opting for one of the back staircases to avoid the crowd. The last thing she wanted was everybody eyeing her in her bathing suit, as she went through the place. Upstairs, she quickly changed into a sundress and sandals, then braided her long blond hair and put it over her shoulder. Walking down the stairs, she took a deep breath and smoothed her braid, trying for a composed look. She knew it would be hard to maintain, but, hey, she was determined to start out that way.

As she walked in, she caught Leia sitting there, an odd look on her face. Lacy walked over, leaned down, and asked, "What's the matter?"

"Indigestion," Leia replied calmly.

"*Right*." Lacy smirked. "You just don't want to say anything."

"Do you know what it is like to be surrounded by as many nursemaids as I have around here?" With a wave of her arm down the table, Leia smirked. "Whoever would have thought that these big brawny men would be so petrified and worried sick over every cough or sneeze?"

"Well, in this case," Lacy noted, "it's potentially with good reason."

"I'm fine," Leia stated firmly. "If anybody goes into labor around here, I'm pretty sure I'll know."

Lacy gave Leia a half smile. "Well, you will eventually. Everybody's just trying to get the jump on you, that's all." With that, she turned and headed to an empty spot at the table. She intentionally didn't look around to see where

Bojan was, just taking the first open chair. Then noted he was staring at her, from directly across the table. She sighed. "Good morning. I hope you slept well."

"I slept fine," he said. "You?"

She nodded. "It took a bit, but I got there eventually." Just then Pia came out with huge platters. She frowned at him. "What's the occasion? Are we celebrating?"

"The men always eat like this," Leia stated calmly. "Particularly when they've just come back from jobs." At that, the platters were passed around, and, before she knew it, a few sausage links were dumped on her plate.

She looked over at Eton. "What if I didn't want that?" she asked, with a frown.

"Eat it anyway," Eton ordered. "You're too skinny."

She sighed. "Are you on Pia's side or something?"

"No, I'm on the side of whoever it was that pointed out you've been losing weight ever since you got here," Eton explained, his voice firm. "We can't have that. You need your energy at all times. If we need to run, we need to know that you're able to run with us." Then he added bacon and several spoonfuls of scrambled eggs on top of her plate.

"Good God," she muttered. "I'll sleep for a week after eating this."

"Yeah, and you can," Eton noted. "It's your day off, so sleep away."

She sighed, then picked up her fork, and, looking around the table, she saw everybody busily chatting among themselves.

Leia caught Lacy's eye and smiled. "See what I mean?"

Lacy nodded. She understood. Everybody was always looking after everybody else. It was sweet, but, at the same time, it was freaking irritating. Still, with half a smile, she dug in, just as Bullard stepped into the room and announced, "We'll be having a meeting after breakfast."

At that, several of the men looked up and asked, "Any reason not to have it now?"

"Yes," Bullard barked. "We will have a private meeting."

"No, you're not," Leia argued, "not if it involves me." She looked over at Bullard, her face flushing. "Everybody is in on it, or nobody is." He glared at her, and she shook her head. "No, that was our agreement. You get to look after me, as long as I'm allowed to stay in the loop. However, if you try keeping secrets from me, I'm going back to work."

He crossed his arms over his chest and continued to glare at her.

She went back to her breakfast, ignoring him, as she picked up another bite of sausage and chewed away thoughtfully, not even looking at him.

But for the sounds of eating, the room was nearly silent, as everybody waited to see what Bullard would do. Then he sighed, his shoulders sagging. "Fine, but you know this is what we do, right?"

"Of course I know it's what you do, and you do it very well. But you won't do it behind my back, without keeping me in the loop."

"Fine," he grumbled, "but not while eating. It will give you indigestion."

"Then you can wait until we're done eating," she replied, with a smile. "Besides, there is sausage, so come and eat."

He looked at the table and frowned. "How come we're having sausage?"

"Because we have company," she declared, looking around.

He sighed, as he threw his huge bulk down onto a chair.

"So because we have company, we get to have sausage? Have I not been asking for sausage for a week?" he muttered.

"We didn't have any until the shipment came in, so stop your bellyaching."

He glared at his wife but rustled several sausages off the platter, just as Eton was busy grabbing several spares.

Bullard now glared at Eton. "Do I get any extra?"

"I don't know. However, if you don't get to the table on time, you know what happens around here," Eton replied, with a smirk. At that, Leia took a sausage off her plate and put it on Bullard's.

"No you don't," he argued. "You're not taking food off your plate to feed me."

"Will you stop? The baby isn't coming anytime soon, so we have time. Would everybody just *chillax*?" At that, an odd silence took over, as she looked up and around. "What?"

"Are you sure it's not coming soon?" Pia asked, as he swapped out a platter. "I think everybody expects you to blow like today or tomorrow."

"It won't be today. It won't be tomorrow. Hell, chances are, it won't be next week either," she complained. "I'm only thirty-four weeks along, so we have another month and a half at least."

At that, Lacy shook her head. "No, you don't," she countered, her voice hard.

At that, Leia looked at her. "So, how long do I have then?" she asked, her voice determined.

Lacy hesitated, then looked over at Bojan, who just shrugged. She looked back over at Leia. "Are you sure you want to know?"

"I want to know," she declared, "and, if nothing else, it will keep the men off my back."

At that, Bojan spoke up. "Details like that aren't always that healthy. If she were to give you a date, it would change your behavior. For example, instead of resting, you would probably work even harder and not get as much rest. No matter when it happens, you need to be taking good care of yourself."

She gasped at that. "That's not fair. At least tell me if it will be early."

"It'll be early," Lacy stated.

The talk at the table stilled. "How early?" Bullard bellowed, staring at her.

"That's the problem," Lacy said. "I can tell you where things are at right now, but I can't guarantee, given more stress or any other changes in her physiological conditions, that it won't change. So, even if I gave you a date and time, it wouldn't necessarily hold true, and then you will say I'm full of shit." She glanced over at Bojan and glared. "You know perfectly well that's what happens every time I end up giving some kind of a premonition."

He muttered, "Much better we don't say anything."

At that, Leia turned slowly to look at him. "You too?"

He shrugged. "Sometimes, yeah."

Leia just stared from one to the other and then turned to Bojan. "Well, you need to give me some idea, so I won't sit here and worry about everybody being upset all the time."

Bullard stared back and forth at the two of them. Then he spoke. "Well, since you two are here, and you're trying to be useful, the least you can do is give us an idea of how much longer we have."

"You should have at least four weeks," Lacy replied. "Now, if you stay calm, maybe even longer. But, if you're overtired and stressed out all the time, it could go the other way."

"We need you at thirty-six weeks at least," Bullard noted, frowning at his wife. "The baby won't be as viable at any less."

"The baby is very viable already," Leia said glaring at him. "And I know perfectly well that we need to get to thirty-six weeks. But it would be helpful to know if it could be thirty-six, thirty-eight, or forty." Leia gave a sideways glance at Lacy. "You and I must have a talk."

Lacy laughed. "Well, we might have to," she declared, with a rueful look over at Bojan, "to clear up a misconception."

"What kind of misconception?" Bullard asked, staring at her suspiciously.

She winced and looked to Bojan for help.

Bojan held up his hands, glaring at Lacy. "Hey, you're the one who brought it up. I would just have kept my mouth shut," he stated.

Lacy added, "Bojan, surely it's better if they know."

"I don't know about that," Bojan hedged. "People get kind of irate over this kind of stuff. Besides, they're doctors, and they should know better."

"I'm almost a doctor," Lacy declared, exasperated. "Besides, it didn't show on any scans." At that, a shocked silence came, and she groaned, then slammed her hand against her mouth. "Damn it." She sighed. "I didn't mean to say that."

"But you did," Bullard stated, his voice soft, almost deadly. "So, whatever it is, we need to know it too."

She groaned again, then looked over at Bojan. "You're really no help at all."

"No, I'm really not," he agreed cheerfully. "Yet now that you've got them all worried, you better spill it."

She switched her gaze to Leia, who was looking at her with shock on her face. "Oh, damn, I'm so sorry. That's the last thing I wanted to do. To start with, nothing is wrong, nothing at all."

Leia settled back a bit, with a slight sigh. "Do you want to explain?"

"Yes, of course. Well, the misconception is that you're having one baby," she cried out. "You're not. You're having twins." At that, a thunderous silence surrounded them.

BOJAN WANTED TO laugh because the look on everybody's face was complete and utter shock. He looked over at Lacy and smiled. It was the one thing he could give her right now. Whatever came out of this, she had definitely surprised them, and he didn't think that happened very often.

"That can't be," Bullard argued. "We've scanned several times."

"Yes, you have, and chances are the next scan would have shown it for sure, but I'm telling you that number two is in there and is being very shy about it all."

"Why though?" Leia inquired.

"I don't know. I haven't asked," Lacy replied.

A series of audible gasps filled the room, and her shoulders sagged even farther. "Oh God, I've had plenty to eat, so I'll grab a coffee and go outside and try to relax." With that, she got up, and, even as she attempted to walk around the table, Bullard got up and glared at her.

"How long have you known?" he asked.

"A couple weeks after I got here, I guess," she muttered. "I thought you guys would have known, but it was for you to figure out. You're also doctors, so I preferred not to say anything. I figured it would show up on the scans, if you didn't figure it out."

"We would have, if there had been any indication at all," Leia admitted, "but honestly, in fairness to you and whatever *messages* you're getting, I'm … confused," Leia said, trying to be delicate about it.

"The scans don't show that," Bullard repeated.

"I know," Lacy agreed. "I've seen the scans myself. Remember?"

"And your explanation for that is what?" Eton asked curiously.

"I don't have an explanation, so we'll just have to wait and see what happens," she muttered. "Now, if you will all excuse me, I definitely need to go digest this meal somewhere else." With that, she stomped off.

Bojan, with a smirk on his face, reached for the sausages she left on her plate, snagging them before the others had a chance to take notice.

Bullard just glared at him. "You agree with her?"

He looked over at him and then nodded. "Yeah, I sure do, but again it won't make a damn bit of difference to us. You guys are the ones with the medical backgrounds."

"It does happen," Leia acknowledged, her voice soft.

Bullard nodded. "It can, for certain, but with our equipment? … Surely with that, we would have known. Sometimes, … no, we should have been able to see it."

"We really depend too much on equipment," Leia noted. "I was much more attuned to the people I helped on my island, with only my senses and my knowledge to guide me. We tend to get lazy and depend far too much on these tools, and they become crutches. I've wondered why I was feeling so tired and worn-out."

"You're thirty-four weeks' pregnant," Bullard noted. "You don't need twins to make that a reality."

She smiled up at him. "I'm just curious about what the answer is though. It doesn't change anything, but, in some ways, it does."

"It does change things," he admitted. "Not a lot, and certainly not in a bad way, so why don't we just wait and see?"

She chuckled. "*Right.* Like you, *right now,* aren't already trying to figure out if you can rush me in for another scan."

He gave her a lopsided grin. "Hey, I'm not against having two sons," he muttered.

"Yeah, how about two daughters?" she challenged.

"If they're anything like you, absolutely."

At that, Bojan sighed. "Wow, is your place just full of this *romance* stuff?"

Ryland laughed. "Yeah, and you might as well get used to it. Ever since we all paired up, it's been like honeymoon haven or something."

Bojan stared at him. "You guys too?"

"Yeah, us too. Several of the women are away on shopping trips in town, a couple partners and the guys are away, one on a job, two are off visiting families. Just couples all over the place here now, whether you like it or not, and the family stuff? … Well, that just got really big."

"It's amazing," Bojan murmured, speaking calmly, trying to keep his voice neutral, but it was hard. "Seems as if it's almost contagious."

"It *is* contagious," Ryland declared in a rough tone of voice. "Yet nobody ever believes us when we say that."

Bojan got up and walked out of the room as well, leaving

an awkward silence behind. He was looking for Lacy and soon found her outside with a book and a cup of coffee in hand, under a large sun umbrella. He sat down beside her, without even asking permission, because he knew she would immediately say no. She raised her focus from her book, then narrowed her eyes and asked, "Why me?"

"I don't know. You're just lucky, I guess."

"No, not really," she argued. "I can't seem to keep my mouth shut."

"I understand the need for sharing in this case, and I don't think it's a bad thing for them to know ahead of time."

"But they don't believe me, and they both have medical backgrounds, or at least have enough medical experience to sort it out themselves. I didn't set out to tell them, but, considering the due-date topic, I figured it might be helpful if they found out," she explained. "Now I feel that maybe I shouldn't have mentioned anything."

"Just let them figure that out, and, if they're not comfortable with it, well, what was it that brought you here in the first place?"

"I'm doing my residency with Leia, and then I'll go back to school in another few months. After that, I wouldn't have to deal with them again I suppose, particularly if I'm not wanted here." At that, she winced.

"Most people won't get angry because you told them a truth, especially since you didn't really understand how they didn't know already."

"Well, that's the thing. I really *didn't* understand how they didn't know. I almost said something the first time I saw her. Then I saw the scans and realized all the discussions were in the singular. All I could think was *How is that even a thing?*"

"Good question, so can you explain it to me?"

She shrugged. "Because the second baby isn't locked in to being here," she began, "and I just didn't want to tell them that."

"Maybe you should though," Bojan suggested, "because now they will be looking for twins, yet that second one isn't as strong, is it?"

"No, it's not," she confirmed, "and an intervention, a physical one, such as a C-section, won't make it any stronger. It's a spirit thing."

He smiled. "You do realize how very odd our conversation is?"

At that, hearing a sound, she noted Dave was behind them.

He walked over, sat down heavily beside them, and asked, "Seriously?"

She looked at him and repeated, "Seriously what?"

"There's a problem with the second baby?" He clasped his hands together, his gaze going from one to the other.

"It's physically viable, but spiritwise it's not very strong. I don't know if that makes any sense to you, but all I can tell you is that the baby won't necessarily be here at the end of the road. I feel terrible about mentioning it because, if we have two healthy babies at the end of the day, Leia would be ecstatic and overjoyed. However, if there's only one, but she's expecting a second, it will be devastating."

Dave stared off in the distance and nodded. "And yet, if they know now, maybe they can do something to improve the odds." At that, he turned and looked at Lacy, with a questioning glance.

"Yes," Lacy replied, "there is. Not that I can tell her how or what or anything," she muttered. "I see and hear things, but they are disjointed, partial glimpses. So that's not always an easy place to be because, just like Bojan, we don't necessarily have answers."

At that, Dave nodded almost absentmindedly. "The thing is," Dave added, "we do have experience with Terkel. So, although what you're saying sounds foreign, we understand that you don't necessarily have answers, even though we want you to." Dave gave her a weak smile. "I would do an awful lot to save them the heartache of losing a child."

Bojan looked at him sharply and then relaxed. "It won't be the same thing as what you went through," he stated.

Dave winced. "Right, that's the awkward part, when the psychic gets to see and to know a whole lot more than everybody else may be comfortable with."

"That goes for us too," she stated, staring at Bojan. "Just like Bojan can't turn it off, I can't turn it off, nor can we turn it off between us."

Dave turned and looked at her, his gaze going from one to the other. "Is that why you two are on the outs? It seems to me that you would make a perfect pair."

"And you're not the first person to mention that, but an element of trust is required, and sometimes, when that doesn't exist or can't exist in harmony, we can't take it any further," she murmured. "So, you talk about having a perfect pair, a soul mate, but what do you do when your soul mate isn't ready or is incapable?" she asked, deliberately not looking at Bojan.

Lacy snorted, then added, "Or when the soul mate or supposed soul mate doesn't see that he's a soul mate or doesn't want to be in a relationship because there's definitely some differences between people. Just because one may have come around in this lifetime to learn something doesn't mean that both are prepared to make the compromises to do the learning together."

Dave's gaze widened as he again glanced from one to the other. "Wow, that really complicates things, doesn't it?"

"You have no idea." Bojan shook his head.

At that, Dave asked Lacy, "Do you mind if I have a talk with Bullard about it?"

"No, I don't mind," Lacy replied. "If there hadn't been a roomful of people, some that I don't even know yet, I would have done it differently. Plus I still need to have that conversation with Leia."

"Do you know what they can do to improve their chances?"

At that, Bojan looked over at her and said, "You might as well tell him."

"I can tell them as much as I know, but I can't guarantee it."

"No, there are no guarantees in life," Dave confirmed, "but I know they will both be willing and ready to do anything they can to keep two healthy babies."

She sighed. "Fine, you talk to them first, and, if they want to talk to me after that, okay. Same for Bojan," she offered, with a wave of her hand. "If Bullard would rather talk to Bojan, he knows the same information I do."

With a shake of his head, Dave got up and disappeared inside.

"Damn it," Lacy muttered. "Now I should just go back to the university."

"Do you always stay here?" Bojan asked.

"At first I didn't, and then, because of all the surgeries, I started staying sometimes. It's hardly a normal residency because such a steady stream of people in need come to the clinic," she murmured. "I've been running my schedule incredibly tight and getting exhausted. So, when they offered me a room and a chance to stay here, I jumped at it. It's been several weeks now. I kind of got settled in, even though another steady stream of Bullard's team come and go—or maybe that's why it worked, I don't know. Still, I've felt comfortable here, and that's not something we feel easily, you know?"

Bojan nodded thoughtfully, as he stared out at the world around them. "No, we don't. We're different, strange even, and that doesn't always sit well with people."

"No," she agreed, feeling tears in the back of her eyes. "I really felt accepted here, and now I've blown it yet again."

"I don't think you've blown anything, and, if you manage to save Leia's life, it won't be an issue."

At that, she looked at him and frowned. "What if all the visions I saw had more to do with the babies than anything else?"

"Why don't you just tell me what you saw," Bojan said, "then I can judge from that. Besides, didn't Terkel agree?"

At that, the expression of relief on her face was evident. "Yes, he did."

"So it wasn't just the babies?"

"No," she replied and felt an odd tickle of a sense. When a commotion came at the back door, they looked up to see both Leia and Bullard coming toward them.

Leia sat down on the footstool and said, "Lacy, we know that this isn't your fault and that it has nothing to do with you, beyond the fact that you're seeing something which is the concern here," she explained, taking a huge breath. "We obviously haven't gotten any confirmation about multiple births, and you seem to have some sort of an explanation as to why that may be."

"I—"

Leia interrupted. "Dave tried to explain, but he was obviously upset, and it came out a bit garbled. We would like to talk to you both about that and wonder if this is why you're seeing my life in danger."

At that, Bojan nodded. "We were just discussing it, but the babies are not the complete answer." Bullard looked at him and frowned. Bojan shook his head. "Something else is going on here, and the babies are an entirely different issue." Then he watched as the pain in Bullard's eyes spread over his face, only to be quickly hidden.

"I get why you would think that," Bojan replied, "but it's not the case." He stopped abruptly, then faced Lacy. "Did you get the timing for that?"

"No, did you pick something up?" she asked Bojan.

He stood up slowly, looked over at Bullard, and asked, "How prepared are you guys for an attack here?"

Bullard straightened, staring at Bojan with a hard gaze. "Dave's watching one area, where our cams pick up movement, mostly at night, probably just some wildlife. Other than that, pretty prepared. Why?"

"An attack is happening somewhere right now," Bojan stated. "It feels like it's your place, yet it's not. … Not sure it's related, but my vision entails some kind of uprising."

At that, Bullard looked at Bojan in shock and muttered, "*Tunisia.*" With only the one word of explanation, he bolted inside.

Leia looked at Bojan and nodded. "Go with him. He has another compound on the Tunisian border."

Shocked, Bojan bolted inside, pausing to give Lacy a quick order. "She needs to know." And, with that, he went after Bullard. There wasn't any sense of urgency to the message he'd received, but, as he stepped inside, he stopped and turned to look around. He felt as if a shadow had walked across his grave. An impending sense of something wrong. *Here.* He slowly glanced around, but he couldn't see anything.

As if sensing he was on to something, the *something's off* premonition drifted away. Bojan went back inside to help Bullard sort out whatever was happening. Bojan couldn't help but wonder if it was all related.

CHAPTER 4

"WHAT DO I need to know?" Leia asked Lacy, her voice shaky.

Lacy rubbed her face, then took a deep breath. "The reason you're not sensing or seeing the second baby in your medical tests is because of something I would call a ghost pregnancy," Lacy began. "So the baby itself has not made a permanent decision at this time."

At that, Leia sucked in her breath. "Holy crap, what does that mean?"

"It means that you could lose the baby because the baby hasn't yet bonded, hasn't resolved in some way to make this a permanent thing."

"So …" Leia stopped and just stared at her. "Is that really a thing?"

"It is really a thing. Sometimes, some babies think that this birth into this life is a good idea, then at the last minute either chicken out or never make a connection as strong as they could have. Therefore, they aren't as strong as they should be, … and they die at birth. In some cases they die in the womb. We've heard of babies dying in vitro. You know that."

"Of course, but I wasn't thinking in those terms with mine."

"No, and I'm feeling really shitty about mentioning it

because, if you had an unexpected twin show up at the end of your pregnancy, you would be ecstatic. Yet, if you have a deceased twin, you'll be heartbroken. If you didn't know about it ahead of time, it just seemed it would be easier somehow."

"I still don't understand how this is something we can't see on the scans."

"Well, when the baby decides and gets a stronger resolve to come into our world, that would then show up on the scan."

"So, even if I have a scan right now, there's a good chance I still won't see the other twin? Is what you're saying?"

"Correct, but, if we can work to strengthen the bond you have with this child, when you do have the next scan, say in another couple of weeks, … it could very well be that the baby will show up on that image."

Leia reached across, gripped Lacy's hands, and whispered, "I really want both children."

Lacy winced. "I know you do, and that's what Bojan was telling me to talk to you about."

"What is that?"

"How you can work to help the child decide."

"And to make it just the way I want?" she asked, with a wry look.

"Exactly. Some things are still beyond us because ultimately it's not your choice. However, I do believe that you can affect the outcome."

"How?" she asked.

Lacy hesitated. "This will be a very simplistic answer, and it probably won't be what you want to hear because you're looking for steps one, two, three to follow," she began, "but really it is just about love. The child hasn't made a decision, hasn't been given whatever it needs in order to lock itself in here. Thus, in that case, it needs to know that you are there for it, that you love it, that you want it, and that you will do whatever it needs to come here and to be part of your family," she explained.

Leia stared at her in shock. "You're right. I don't like that answer at all." Looking out to the compound, she muttered, "It's too simplistic. Of course I love this baby. I want them both to be here with me. But why would my other twin not want that too?"

"Lots of reasons can be given. It could be that there's a defect or that the life the baby sees ahead doesn't have the life lessons this baby needs to learn, and so the shy twin is not sure that this is where the baby wants to be at this time. It could be that the baby will be born with a disability that will make life too hard. Or a disability where the baby won't survive." Lacy paused, then continued. "Some people believe that, when souls reincarnate, they make agreements, contracts to come on the other side, and some of those are not for its own learning but for the learning for others."

Leia just stared at her.

"I know this is not a discussion you thought you would have today," Lacy admitted, with a groan. "And I'm so sorry because it's not a discussion I should be having with you either."

"Why is that?" Leia asked, her tone rough.

"Because this is really about you and the baby, and if there's anything that you can do to help that baby feel more secure and well-loved, and you can influence whatever is going on in that baby's life, then you need to go lie down, meditate, and talk to both of those children. You didn't know there were two before, and you may not consider it a case where the second child is listening to you and being jealous. Regardless that baby's still undecided. Otherwise that baby would have made its presence known."

Leia just couldn't find the words to say anything.

"I get it. It sounds like complete malarkey to you," Lacy noted, "and this is why I don't have many friends."

At that, Leia laughed. "Good God, girl, if you know stuff like this about other people, life can't be all that easy."

"No, it isn't," she agreed. "I've seen women with dead babies in their wombs," she murmured. "Nothing is easy about knowing that kind of information, and worse knowing you can do absolutely nothing to help them."

"What do you feel around me?" Leia asked.

"For what it's worth, I don't see or feel death around you." Such a look of relief crossed Leia's face that Lacy immediately reached out and added, "But, having said that, I still just can't be sure how this will end up."

"No, that's fine. I get it," Leia said, now sitting up straighter. "And now that I know, believe me. I am very eager to go meet this new addition in my life." With that, she waddled off.

Lacy stared after her, wondering if she'd done the right thing.

She sagged into place on the lounge chair, wondering what she was supposed to do about any of this. Just as she decided she wanted to nap and to try to forget the incredibly stressful morning, she heard an odd sound nearby. She turned and saw nothing, as far as she could see, but, as she went to relax again, something felt *off*.

She snatched her phone and hit Dial, not realizing until she heard Bojan's voice that it was his number. "Did he say the attack was in Tunisia?"

"I don't know," he said in frustration. "Yes and no."

"Whatever that means, this right here, I don't feel right," she muttered.

"Hang on. I'll be right there."

She sighed, putting down her phone. She looked around again but still found nothing worrisome. Yet that same odd whisper of warning floated in her brain.

Unnerved, she bolted to her feet and raced toward the kitchen door. Just as she got there, she heard another odd sound. It was a *ping*, an odd *ping* sound, but then she stared around, not understanding what had happened. Her knees came out from under her, and she slowly slipped to the ground right at the back door. She heard shouts, as Bojan grabbed her, right before her head hit the tiled floor.

"Hey, what's going on?" he asked.

She opened her mouth and tried to speak. Then, just like that, came blackness.

BOJAN LET OUT a shout, as he bent down and quickly collected Lacy in his arms, racing toward the surgery suite, his mind cataloguing what had just happened, even as he yelled again for help. Chairs scattered, and people bolted toward him, with Bullard quickly taking charge.

"Get her to the operating table." He looked at Bojan and asked, "What the hell happened?"

"I don't know," he roared, as he raced toward the surgery suite. "She called and told me that she felt off like, that something was up. When I got there, she was leaning against the back door, and she's obviously been shot."

At that, the rest of the team scattered, heading outward across the property.

Bojan didn't know where they were going, and he didn't give a damn. He just wanted to ensure that whoever had shot her was caught. He laid her down gently on a clean operating table, grateful that Bullard had the facilities here to take care of most emergencies.

Leia wobbled in right behind Bullard. "Let me take a look at her."

Bullard glared at her. "You could just sit down, you know?"

"I could," she agreed, "but I've certainly seen my share of bullet holes."

"You and me both," Bullard muttered, as he quickly checked Lacy over. "It went through her side," he noted, checking out the wound at her belly. "Any closer and it would have done some serious damage, but it looks like the bullet missed the major organs," he muttered, as he bent closer.

Bojan stayed close, watching as both Bullard and Leia worked on Lacy. "How bad is it?" Bojan asked. Leia just shot him a look, and he shut up. It always amazed him how some people had that ability, but, given the circumstances, he was hardly one to argue right now.

Finally Bullard gave a sigh and stepped back, looking over at Bojan. "She was damn lucky."

Bojan nodded. "I got that message already," he snapped, his gaze hard. "You're still not telling me anything new."

"She'll be fine. She will be damn sore. We will have to go in and make sure nothing else was hurt and nothing major was ripped. The bleeding is still ongoing, so the bullet might have nicked something. You need to get the hell out of here, and we will scrub up and take care of this. Go find that bullet," he ordered.

Bojan stepped back and stared down at Lacy, but Bullard wasn't having it.

"Go on," he repeated. "My team's out there looking for the shooter, so you need to go find the bullet. She's doesn't have one in her body, so you better find it."

With that, Bojan nodded. "You look after her," he ordered.

"Done, now go find that damn bullet."

With that, Bojan quickly raced back outside again, stopping at the rear doorway. It didn't take much effort to find it, as the bullet had slammed into the door itself, splintering wood all over the place. He bent down and, using his pocketknife, quickly dug it out of the wood frame and put it in a small container he had snagged from the kitchen. With that in hand, he headed back to Bullard.

Just as he walked into the surgery, Leia looked up and glared at him. "Nobody comes in here while we're operating," she muttered.

"*Great*," Bojan said, standing at the edge of the doorway, watching as they worked on Lacy. "I found the bullet."

"Good, take it to Dave," Bullard replied, without looking back. "He'll run ballistics."

Bojan's eyebrows shot up at that, but he turned and obediently headed out to find Dave. There was a good chance he was out looking for the shooter too. But, as Bojan walked into the main control room here in the compound, Dave looked up from monitoring a series of massive screens.

"Before you ask, we haven't found the shooter yet," Dave shared.

"No, but I've got the bullet, if that helps."

Dave's gaze lit up with interest, and he held out his hand. "I'll run it. Pretty ballsy move to attack somebody in this compound."

"Unless it was someone who doesn't really understand who is here," Bojan suggested. "Not everybody knows this is Bullard's main compound, right?"

"Anybody who's done any kind of online research on the location would sure as hell have figured it out, although they may not know just what doing something like this on Bullard's property would mean. Regardless, shooting somebody in anybody's backyard isn't good for business. And Bullard has already added a layer of hired guns around the perimeter, especially with us now actively searching for our shooter. Those guys will remain on guard, until we have the shooter in hand."

"I don't think the shooter really gave a shit about business," Bojan noted. "If you think about it, he shot and ran."

"You didn't hear anything as you stepped out?"

"No, she was right there on the ground in front of me, so I grabbed her before she went all the way down, and I ran her to the clinic. It was obvious that she was hurt, and she also knew something was wrong before it happened. By the time I got to her, the blood was oozing out all over the place."

"Yeah, I've got to go clean that up too," Dave muttered.

"Let me grab some photos of the scene first."

At that, Dave nodded. "Don't know if it will do much good, but go for it. Let me know when you are through, so I can get it cleaned up before any of the other women get home."

"Are they all due in today?"

"Not if we've got a shooter on the loose," Dave replied.

"Bullard had me put this place on lockdown, letting every-body know it's not safe."

"Right, I guess that makes sense."

"It's all about keeping everybody safe," Dave noted, scanning the multiple screens for any signs. "We have enough enemies that we can't be lax about our security."

"Yet how did this happen?"

"Oh, don't worry. We'll be on to that pretty-damn fast," he snapped, his voice hard.

With that reminder, Bojan headed to the kitchen and stepped outside and quickly took some photos. However, as Dave had said, not a whole lot to see. As Bojan stepped back into the kitchen, he crossed paths with Pia.

Pia headed outside with a big bucket and a mop and shooed him away. "I'll take care of this. You go look after her."

"They just kicked me out of the surgery." Bojan groaned, glaring at him.

Pia nodded. "In that case, the whiskey is in the office. Go grab a shot." When Bojan hesitated, Pia glared at him. "This is my domain, now go."

With a sigh, Bojan stepped out of the way and turned to look around at the property surrounding him. Surely there was a way to find out who had been here.

He quickly stepped out onto the lawn and headed to where the shooter must have fired from. Studying the grounds, he looked for any sign of a trespasser. Only as he stood here in the far back section did he note that, whoever had been here, had to have been on top of the fence or in a tree. With that thought, he quickly scooted up the closest tree and took a look. It took him about forty minutes to check out various locations before he was satisfied that he was at the spot the shooter had fired from. He could only judge by the trajectory line, after having seen the wound, but this location appeared to be the closest he could get to his shooter's vantage point.

When someone down below called out to him, Bojan looked through the boughs of the tree to find Ryland. Bojan quickly climbed down and pointed. "He was up there."

"Any signs?"

"Nothing," Bojan muttered in frustration. "But who the hell would even know you can see the pool from here?"

"That's part of what we have to sort out. If it's somebody potentially after Bullard, then they may have researched this compound quite well. Although we've buried as much online information as we can on us and our operations, once you put enough together, it's pretty hard to keep the world from being alerted to this location."

"I get that, but these trees are high enough that somehow he must have climbed up and gotten above the security cams and triggers."

"I'll check that out in the control room when I go inside," Ryland stated, as he studied the dividing wall in front of them. "We don't generally get anybody on this side of the property. Since we nearly lost Bullard, we haven't double-checked this area that closely. We'll need to do another full round on security issues here," he muttered. "That should never have slipped our attention."

"I'm sure it's somebody's job, but, with so much to do, attention gets focused on the highest need at the moment, or sometimes people come and go, and something like this doesn't get assigned to someone else."

Ryland looked at Bojan and nodded. "That's quite true. We did have a grounds person who was looking after all this, somebody Bullard has worked with for many years. Maybe I'll give him a call."

"A call to see where he was, to see if anybody has asked him about this compound, or to ask if he could come and tune it up?"

"Good point. All of the above," he replied, keeping his voice quiet. "We'll give him the benefit of the doubt and talk to him when he gets here."

"Sounds good," Bojan said, turning to look around. "From this edge of the property, it's not that hard to access the compound."

At that, the two men climbed the tree, then went over the dividing wall into the neighbors' yard. And just as easily, the two men scaled the wall, jumped for the tree, and dropped back down into Bullard's compound.

"Damn, that was way too easy," Ryland muttered. "We'll have a meeting over this when everybody gets in. How is Lacy?" They both walked back to the compound.

"She's alive, and they're still in surgery, patching her up. The bullet went clear through. I found it in the doorframe and gave it to Dave."

"Good. Not that it will necessarily do that much for us, but anything we can find is information we'll eventually use. How did you happen to be going out there to Lacy?" Ryland asked curiously.

"She phoned me and told me something didn't feel right, so I booked it. If she was calling for me, something was way wrong. She was obviously racing toward the house when it happened, so she must have seen something or felt she needed to head for safety. She was shot right at the back door."

"Damn." Ryland shook his head. "We normally would

have an awful lot of women here."

"Another thing I was wondering about," Bojan added. "Obviously Lacy is not expecting, but, if somebody didn't know about the pregnancy anyway, could the shooter have been after Leia?"

Ryland came to a dead stop, then turned and stared at him. "I hate to think of that being a possibility, but I guess it's something we have to look at."

"They both have the same stature, outside of the pregnancy," Bojan muttered, "and they're both blonds."

At that, Ryland nodded. "No, I hear you. It's possible it was a case of mistaken identity. It's possible that there was no mistake about it or that they didn't care who it was. His victim could have been anybody on Bullard's compound, as far as the shooter was concerned. All equally offensive options and not something we like to think about." As the two men walked back, they stopped at the steps, and Bojan pointed out what he saw and where.

"Okay, so that tree was probably the best detail we will get," Ryland noted. "So now we need her to wake up and to tell us if she has any insights into what happened."

"Wouldn't that be nice," Bojan replied, his voice hard. "They won't even let me in there to check on her."

"No, they're very protective about surgery," Ryland said, looking over at Bojan. "You wouldn't get into a surgery suite in any other medical facility either, and infection in that wound is the last thing Lacy needs. Try to understand where they're coming from and give them a pass."

"I don't have a problem with that, as long as they're keeping her alive. But I also need to talk to her and need to find out what the hell tipped her off and if she saw anything."

"If he fired from that tree, as you suspect, chances are she didn't get a look at anything. It could have just been a sound or maybe nothing, maybe just instincts. If her instincts are on high alert, and she was not distracted …" Ryland sent a sideways glance to Bojan.

"Generally that's not something that would apply," Bojan stated, frowning.

"Maybe not, but she's definitely been a little rattled since you've been here."

"Considering what she brought up over breakfast, I'm not surprised she's been upset and feeling pretty rough about things."

"I'm not exactly sure what the problem is with the pregnancy, but I gather there's something?"

"Apparently there's a second baby that's not doing as well as it could be—or something along those lines," he shared, with a shrug. "Lacy felt terrible even bringing it up."

Ryland nodded slowly.

Bojan added, "But, if something could be done, and she didn't say anything, she would feel terrible too. It's one of those *damned if you do, damned if you don't* situations."

"Right," Ryland replied, "but Bullard and Leia are solid and have top-notch medical experience, so, if there is a problem, I'm sure they can fix it."

"Maybe, but they're also the parents, and that adds in an emotional layer that nobody really sees. You don't know how it affects you, not until you're in that situation."

"That's true. We never really thought we'd see Bullard like this anyway," Ryland noted. "However we're all really rooting for them."

"Of course, and I don't know Leia's history or anything regarding the pregnancy or the potential for more down the road, but, if there are two viable babies, we want to keep it that way."

"Wouldn't that be something," Ryland noted, with a sigh.

"What about you?" Bojan asked, looking at him. "I hear you've got a partner too."

His expression changed, and instantly he was beaming. "I do, indeed," he declared, cheering up. "She's back in Australia right now, settling things up, and getting ready to move her things over. She needed to go back for some recertification, so she decided it was a good time to sort out the move and to spend time with friends and family, before officially moving here. She'll return in another week or so. … It can't happen fast enough for me."

"It's serious then?"

"Oh, yes, very serious," he confirmed. "Absolutely. I haven't asked her to marry me, but it's one of those things that's a given."

"Is there such a thing?" Bojan asked him. "It seems to me that, as far as women are concerned, nothing is really a given."

"I can't argue with you on that one, but I sure as hell hope it's considered a given in this case," Ryland stated. "We've been together since we found each other, and this is the longest we've been apart."

Just then Bullard called out to them.

They stepped in through the kitchen and headed toward the massive dining room, where everybody seemed to congregate. Bullard stood there, his hands on his hips, glaring at Bojan.

"You're pissed off at me, why?" Bojan asked.

"I'm not," Bullard said, shaking his head. "I'm pissed off

at the whole situation. Lacy will be fine, though she's still out cold. When she wakes up, she will be damn sore, and she won't be doing anything for the next few days. We've had to stitch her up but didn't have to do too much in the way of opening the wound to clean things out and to look for internal bleeding. She will be just fine though," he repeated, holding up his hands, as Bojan immediately headed to the surgery suite. "Did you hear me say she's unconscious?"

"Yeah, I sure did," he said, as he continued walking toward Lacy.

Bullard glared at his back and yelled, "You will be difficult, won't you?"

He turned, stared at Bullard, and asked, "And if that were Leia?"

At that, Bullard's eyebrows shot up. "No question where I would be. However, my understanding is that you two don't have that kind of relationship."

Bojan shot him a dirty look and turned to walk out, hearing Bullard's laughter behind him.

"Nothing like a reality check, is there?" Bullard yelled.

"No reality check," Bojan called back. "Besides, she's damn-near family." Bojan knew that they didn't understand, but really, who the hell would? Their situation was too damn complicated to make any kind of sense.

Moments later, he walked into the surgery suite to find Leia standing there, adjusting the blanket over Lacy.

She looked up, glared at him, and ordered, "You scrub up if you're coming in here."

He nodded, noting this wasn't the main surgery room but a little recovery room off to the side. "How is she?" he asked, as he quickly washed up.

"She will be sore, really sore, and weak of course, but

she'll be fine. Post-operative infection is always a concern, so we'll have to watch that carefully, as always," she explained. "Bullard, on the other hand, is not faring so well. The fact that Lacy got shot here on the property has him livid."

"I know. I just talked to him," Bojan stated. "Mostly I think it's because he's worried about you."

"Not just me," she corrected, with a smile. "Anybody involved on the property. He takes his responsibilities very seriously."

"I'm pretty sure I know how the shooter got in, and I don't know if it was on the schedule to fix up that dividing wall on the east side or not, but it definitely needs to move up on the to-do list."

"I think he did mention something about it, though it's not been an issue before. That particular field was pretty inaccessible on the far east side, but there had also been another wall, a taller one, on that adjacent property. The owner took it down for some reason recently, and now it's left us more vulnerable on that side," she murmured.

Bojan nodded, not really understanding, but willing to believe there was a reason for the security slip. Turning his attention to Lacy, he asked, "How long will she be like this?"

"Another couple of hours. Then, once she's awake, I don't want her doing anything but bed rest for several more days for sure, if not a full week."

"Got it. That will be interesting because she won't take that very well."

"No, she sure won't," Leia agreed, with a knowing smile, "but it is what it is." She looked over at him. "Now, if you have any kind of ability to heal or anything along those lines with the energy work you do, I suggest you start applying yourself. I'll leave you here to spend a few minutes with her.

Do not touch her physically, and, if she wakes up, don't do anything except restrain her, and I will be here in seconds," she muttered. "I'm heading to the bathroom. Nothing like doing surgery with a huge belly like this, but, even worse, the bathroom is never close enough."

He grinned as she waddled off; then his smile fell away as he looked down at Lacy. He sensed her energy reaching, searching the ethers, looking for something, and he knew perfectly well what it was.

As he stared at her, seeing her looking so lost and so very fragile, he gave in almost immediately. He reached out with his own energy, gently touching hers. Instantly she latched on, and their energy entwined with a sense of coming home.

He whispered, as he stared down at her, "What am I to do with you?"

He knew there was no *singular* answer; there never had been, just confusion. And yet the one primary answer was without question, the same as it had always been. They were meant to be together, yet he was holding back as he always had. Mostly to protect her, though look what had happened. Even here, a place that was far more secure than most, still he had failed to protect her. He studied the pallor of her skin, wishing he'd been able to do something, anything to stop that damn bullet. Then remembering what Leia had suggested, he closed his eyes and started pouring healing energy into Lacy's system.

She was like a dry well and sucked up everything he poured her way. As she absorbed it with open arms, he winced, knowing with clarity that their ability to stay apart from each other and to maintain separate lives would no longer be possible. Yet no way he could withhold any help at this moment, not when she needed him the most.

Closing his eyes and accepting whatever was coming, he continued to pour as much energy as he could funnel into her body and into her heart. He didn't even worry about the wound. That would take care of itself. In this moment, it was all about her heart.

CHAPTER 5

L ACY OPENED HER eyes slowly, the pain in her side diminishing down to a weird buzz. She glanced around, frowning.

"Don't move," Leia ordered, immediately at her side.

Lacy stared at her in confusion. "What happened?" she asked, as she stifled a yawn. "Why am I so tired?"

At that, Leia gave her an odd look. "How's the pain?"

Lacy assessed it, then shrugged. "I'm not sure what happened, but painwise, I feel pretty good."

"On a scale of one to ten, what is your pain level?"

"One or two, maybe," she replied, looking up at Leia. "Why? What happened?"

Leia pulled up a chair, then sat down beside her. "You were shot."

Lacy looked at her in astonishment, then tried to bolt upright, only to have Leia push her back down again.

"Don't move," Leia ordered, then looked at her curiously. "When you moved just now, how was the pain?"

Lacy shrugged. "Not much at all. Why?"

She nodded thoughtfully. "Well, I did leave Bojan here with you for a little while."

She snorted at that. "Bojan wouldn't have helped."

"Oh, I think he did more than help," Leia countered, "unless you have a group of healers somewhere you can tap into."

At that, Lacy winced. "Definitely a lot of healers are out there, so maybe Bullard pulled some strings to bring them in or something, but I doubt it."

At that, the door opened, and Bullard walked in, Bojan behind him.

She looked up at Bojan and frowned, and he frowned in return. She almost smiled at the speed of his response. She turned her gaze to Bullard. "Leia just told me that I was shot."

Bullard nodded, his hands shoved into his pockets as he walked closer. "What do you remember?"

She frowned, closing her eyelids—which is how they wanted to be anyway—then tried to think back. "I was out by the pool," she murmured. "Something felt off. It's hard to even describe what it was. I think I called Bojan, didn't I?" she asked, her eyelids flying open to look at him.

Bojan nodded. "You said something felt wrong, and I came running, but, as I raced to the back door, you were crumpled against it, shot in your side." He motioned with his hands toward her belly.

She placed her hands there, feeling the bandage, her gaze going to Leia, who nodded in confirmation. "I can't be too badly hurt," she noted, with a shrug. "I can't feel anything really." Then she smiled. "Unless you've got wonderful drugs or something."

"We do have wonderful drugs, as you know," Leia stated in a dry note. "However, you've definitely got something else going on there." Then Leia turned to look at Bojan, with a raised eyebrow.

Bojan didn't look at Leia, keeping his focus on Lacy. "What can you tell me about who was out there?"

"I can't tell you anything," she said. "I know you're looking for answers, but I don't have any to give you. I told you all there is."

"Oh, you have the answers," Bojan argued calmly. "You're just not remembering them yet."

She groaned, closed her eyelids again, and moaned. "*Ugh*, back to that again."

"Yeah, back to that again," Bojan repeated, with a nod. "There are memories in your head, and you just have to pull them forward. Stop trying to block them."

"Well, right now I don't really feel like pulling them forward—or whatever I can do," she muttered, staring at him. "When did it happen?"

"Less than an hour ago," Bojan replied, as he double-checked his watch and then shook his head. "Make that four hours ago."

"Really? So I've lost most of the afternoon?"

Bojan nodded. "Yes, and we really need to know if you can tell us more."

"I just felt something wrong, so I called you. Then there was that … that weird urgent need to get up and to move. I got up and raced to the door. Then I felt a weird pain. I didn't know what it was. After the blackness took over, there was just … nothing."

Bojan nodded. "You heard the shot, probably felt the tug, and didn't really realize what was going on. Then the shock and the pain would have hit you. That's probably what knocked you out—or self-preservation maybe," he muttered, looking at her thoughtfully.

"Oh, I don't know about that because wouldn't self-preservation have had me running for the hills? If they shot me once, they could just as easily have shot me a second time," she murmured. "Obviously whoever was out there had a solid bead on me. It's a little disconcerting to think that we can't even sit out around the pool without somebody trying to shoot us."

"That's why we're trying to get to the bottom of this," Bullard declared. "I can't have anybody here put in danger, particularly not after your warning."

"Yeah, my warning about Leia." Then she turned toward Leia and said, "And thanks for patching me up."

"Well, it was a two-person job," she replied. "I'm struggling to reach the table as it is, but Bullard is a pretty handy guy, especially when it comes to stitching up bullet wounds."

Lacy smiled. "So I owe you both a thank-you."

"You were on my property when it happened," Bullard stated briskly. "So I hardly think any thank-you should be coming my way. I'm just pissed that it happened in the first place."

Lacy yawned. "Well, the longer I lie here, the more unhappy I'm getting about the whole deal too." Lacy sank back down again and added, "I'm tired, so I don't know whether that's the medication or something else." Lacy yawned again. "I'm pretty whacked."

"It's the medication," Bojan pointed out. "You need to get some sleep."

"That would be nice," she muttered. "Maybe you guys can let me sleep now, since I really don't have anything to offer." She yawned yet again, then closed her eyelids and heard the sounds of everybody else moving away. She went under again, quickly succumbing to exhaustion.

WHEN LACY WOKE the next time, she yawned, trying to roll over. Almost instantly the pain slammed into her. She gasped and winced. "Jesus, what the hell is that?"

"You were shot," Bojan said at her side.

"But it didn't hurt before."

"You didn't feel the pain when you woke up before because I stopped it."

She froze, then glared at him. "And then what? You don't feel like stopping it now?"

"No, but I'm afraid that if you have no pain, you'll do too much thrashing around, like you did before."

She glared at him. "That's hardly fair."

"Really? If you weren't hurting right now, what would you be doing?"

"I don't know. I haven't had a chance to think about it." Still, she knew he was right. She would definitely be doing too much. "You could keep it at a minimum."

"Sure, but you can also do that for yourself," he stated, with that hooded gaze.

"I suppose you didn't tell them you did anything, did you?"

"No, I didn't, and you know why."

"I know, and it is something we have to keep in control at all times. It's one of the reasons I went into becoming a doctor."

"Why? So you could use your skills outright?"

"Partly that but partly because then I wouldn't be afraid of having skills. I mean, I'll have to moderate my language so people don't know, but I should at least give people the benefit of what I can do."

"Well, right now you're the one in need, so you can fix yourself," Bojan stood up and walked toward the door.

At that, she turned back to him and said, "Still afraid, *huh*?"

He just glared at her and left.

She sagged back, wincing. Now that he had withdrawn at least a portion of the energy that was helping her, the pain had definitely kicked in much more than she wanted.

Just then Leia walked in, studied her, and asked, "How's the pain?"

"It sucks," she muttered.

Leia laughed. "Well, a certain amount of pain is to be expected."

"Sure, but I don't have to like it. … Sorry, I don't mean to be grumpy."

"No worries. I can give you some pain meds, if you like," she offered.

Lacy thought about it and shook her head. "No. I'm afraid I'll wind up trying to do too much."

"That's what I was expecting." Leia hesitated, then turned to look at her patient. "Can you reduce your own pain?"

"I can do a little bit of it," Lacy replied, "but it takes an awful lot of my energy to do so. It would be easier if it was somebody else's energy, since I'm expending as much as I can trying to heal already. It's a tradeoff, you know?"

"Right." Leia didn't say anything for a long moment but then asked, "So, Bojan can do it too, can't he?"

Lacy stared up at Leia. "It's really his tale to tell."

"He doesn't need to say very much," Leia noted, with a wry look. "I left him alone with you for a just a few minutes, while I went to the bathroom. When I came back, you were sound asleep and resting comfortably. Then you woke up without any pain."

Lacy sighed. "But now he took away the pain block because he was afraid I would do too much if I felt no pain, and that would make my wound worse." She shook her head. "That's Bojan's measure of the right thing to do."

At that, Leia laughed. "Not a bad strategy though. You've both used whatever healing energy was available, and, since your wound is not fully healed, you can easily cause more damage."

"Yeah, I get it," Lacy muttered.

"It's really amazing that you guys can do something like this at all," Leia said, studying Lacy carefully. "Wish I knew more."

"We can do it sometimes, not always, and certain repercussions are involved," Lacy shared. "It's one of the reasons I wanted to go into medicine because then I can utilize my gifts to some degree, without it raising alarms."

"And yet, if you can take away pain, as Bojan seemed to do, that will raise eyebrows."

"Yes, it's possible, and I would have to be very conservative with it. I don't know how it will work out in practice. I just thought it would give me a better opportunity to help people," Lacy explained. "It's also very inconsistent. Some would say the inconsistency is a lack of skill or control. I don't know what is involved just yet, but I notice that, when I'm a little more emotionally involved, … it's much harder."

Leia nodded. "That makes a whole lot of sense. However, if you have a healing gift, it would be a shame to not use it. Just a thought to hold on to."

"May be a shame, but, if people find out, it's more than a shame. It becomes a huge burden," she stated boldly. "Not to mention all the trouble it brings. We can't help everybody, and I can't even maintain it for a long time period, so it's a matter of potentially helping somebody long enough to get them more help, or I could envision thwarting an emergency situation. I might do enough to get them through something," she added. "I can't save everybody or many people at all. So, in a way, it's better if you don't even think about us doing something like that because it can't be counted on. Not for long. Not for every circumstance."

Leia sat back, a pensive expression on her face, as she contemplated what Lacy had told her. "And, of course, the pressure is always on you, isn't it?"

"It always feels that way. Bojan would never acknowledge what he can do or cannot do."

"That is a given, and I have to respect his privacy over that too," Leia said wistfully. "Still, to think that you guys have the ability to help at that level—"

"Yet, not everybody—you've got to remember that. So the minute you expect us to help, and we can't, you'll feel like we've let you down, as will we." Lacy sighed. "Not an easy way to live."

"No, of course not," Leia agreed. "It's terrible to even think that you would feel guilty for something like that, when you'd done your best to try and help. I can see how that could be misconstrued."

"Exactly, so we can still do some healing, though it's mostly energy manipulation. Such as, in the case of my own healing, I can do something to remove some of the pain. Bojan knows I can do that, and he also knows I can't do all of it. I can't just block it off and carry on and expect my body to heal. I can't just heal overnight and get up and walk away tomorrow. He's counting on the fact that I can do enough to keep myself content and stable."

"But not feel so well that you run into trouble," Leia

added, with a big smile. "It's kind of a brilliant strategy."

"It really is," she grumbled. "As for the patient, that rest is important, but, as for the doctor, somebody who's up and at it, moving around all the time, you also know how hard it is to give ourselves that kind of rest, despite our best intentions. In this circumstance, I really don't have much choice."

Leia laughed. "No, you don't. What I'll do is give you a hand to get you up to your room, and we'll set you up with someone to help when you need it. You'll get some bed rest and relax in a quieter, more comfortable space, while the rest of the crew is running around with their hair on fire, trying to find the shooter."

"Yeah, I'm totally okay to be away from all that chaos," Lacy murmured. "It doesn't sound like much fun."

"No, and Bullard's on the rampage because you were shot on his property, and, in his mind, under his protection. Of course, if you had anything to offer in terms of information, you know how badly they need it. His Tunisian location had Hsome unrest nearby in these last few days, but that didn't end up involving his other African compound there. More that it happened outside and involved a few of the contractors he uses on a regular basis. We haven't had much chance to follow up on that yet. Things are a little busy here."

"Yeah, wouldn't that be nice if I had information," Lacy replied, with a sarcastic tone. "I really don't remember much, and, even if I did, I don't think it would be of any value because I didn't hear anything really. It was just a feeling, a fleeting sense of being watched, and no way you can track that."

"Fair enough. Let's go," Leia said, as she pulled back the sheets on the hospital bed.

Lacy slowly sat up, realizing that she was mostly undressed. "Did you put me in a hospital gown?"

"Yes. You were covered in blood, and we had to get both your tops and bottoms off," she replied. "I just cut them off. Luckily you were just wearing the sundress, so I snipped the straps, and we pulled it off. It's a bloody mess, but you might get it out. Your underwear didn't fare that well."

"Well, in the grand scheme of things, that won't be an issue," she noted, as she slowly stood up, wincing as the pain kicked in. "Damn," she muttered. "I liked being shot a whole lot better without the pain."

"Yeah, and you looked like a real badass for a while there too," Leia shared, pushing a wheelchair closer, then helping her into it.

"I'm not loving Bojan's logic so much now."

"No, but it makes good sense, even though it feels like tough medicine at the moment."

Slowly they made their way up to Lacy's room. When she finally managed to get on her bed, it was with relief and no argument.

"See? The fact that you're not even arguing or protesting means this is where you belong," Leia stated.

"I know. I know. I hear all that logic flowing through you. It's just hard right now," she added irritably, "because the pain is worse than expected."

"I can give you painkillers."

"I know, but we also know that they don't really help in the healing process, so I'm better off if I don't have it."

"Only as long as you can keep the pain moderated," Leia stressed, a lecturing tone to her voice. "Because, if the body is in pain, it won't rest either, and no rest hampers healing as well."

"Absolutely." Once Lacy was under the sheets, her eyelids closed, she whispered, "I'll just see if I can knock back some of this pain a little bit and sleep, if I can. Thank you for everything."

"Absolutely," Leia said, hesitating before she left the room. "Are you planning on sticking around for when I … have the baby?" Then she quickly corrected it. "The babies, I mean?"

Lacy opened her eyes, looked over at her friend, and replied, "That depends on if you want me around."

"I definitely want you around," Leia confirmed.

"But what if I can't help in any way?"

Leia smiled. "It's fine and I understand," she declared, "but I can't help but think that it's better to have you here than not, for many reasons. One being, if the one twin is in trouble, maybe you can do something. However, I definitely understand there's no guarantee, and I would never want you to feel pressured or responsible in any way, no matter what happens."

"If you understand and accept that much," Lacy muttered, with a strained smile, "then I would love to be here. I can't say I'm going anywhere anytime soon anyway." And, with that, she yawned.

Leia chuckled. "We'll talk when you feel better." She closed the door behind her, as she walked out.

Lacy closed her eyelids, focusing on pain relief, and, before long, fell asleep.

DOWNSTAIRS IN THE kitchen, with a cup of coffee in hand, Bojan listened to the plan Bullard had set out for trying to find the shooter. Bojan didn't care what Bullard did; Bojan would go on his own and find this asshole. And that was mostly because somebody had attacked Lacy. It was one thing for people to backtalk her, to question her, or to be annoyed with her, but to attack her? … No way. If anybody got on her bad side, it would be him. But he for damn sure wouldn't stand by while some asshole got away with shooting her.

As Leia waddled in, he winced at the size of her belly, then turned his gaze toward Ryland, who saw the wince and grinned. But he kept his mouth shut, which was a damn good thing. She walked closer, then chose to sit down beside Bojan.

"She's asleep now, or she should be. She was yawning. I put her in her room, and she will stay there for the rest of the day." He nodded but didn't say anything. Leia continued. "The pain is not good but manageable, and it's keeping her in bed."

"Good," he snapped. "That's where she should stay."

"As if you would do in the same situation, right?" Bullard joked.

Bojan stared at him, then admitted, "No, probably not." But he had a method of keeping himself from having to stay down when he was hurt. At the same time, he also knew the toll that took on his own health.

At that, he listened to the conversation, yet waited as Leia kept looking over at him, as if she wanted to ask something else. He hoped that she didn't say anything right now, and he built the energy wall a little bit thicker and stronger, hoping she'd get the message. Thankfully she didn't bring up the topic, until later that evening, when one of the groups that had been out searching came back, having found nothing.

With their report—or lack thereof—in progress, she turned and looked at him. "May I speak with you for a few minutes?"

He frowned but knew in no way would he deny her this opportunity to say what was on her mind. Not only was she his host while he was here, she was one of the people he was here to protect. With a quick nod, he stood. She got up and walked into one of the other little rooms. The place was full of them. As he walked in behind her, he leaned against the closed door and said, "No."

"No?" She looked at him. "What?"

"No."

"How did you know what I wanted to ask?" She was clearly aghast.

"Because everybody asks for the same thing."

Understanding crossed her face as she nodded, and her shoulders sagged. "Right. You have a skill, and you can't help everybody."

"Right. I have a skill. I can't help everybody. I can't help a lot of people. Sometimes I can't help anybody," he snapped. "There is an odd relationship between Lacy and me, and that is the reason I could help her. Now, I don't have a clue of the dynamism here, but it's possible it might work for you. I just don't know," he admitted, trying to close the subject. "Earlier today was an emergency situation, and Lacy's doing much better, so I've withdrawn all further assistance for her."

"Of course and I get that." Leia eyed him curiously. "The fact is, the two of you are bonded in a way that nobody else can even understand, but aren't you curious as to what you can do together?"

"It's the same way you and Bullard are bonded," he noted reluctantly. "It's just not necessarily a bond we are choosing to continue with."

"That just blows me away," she replied. "I would have given anything to have somebody be the other half of my heart or to at least care for me. And I know she feels the same way, so I think it's you who's holding back, and I struggle to understand why."

"Leia, … forgive me for being direct, but it's not for you to understand," he declared, his voice tight.

She sighed. "That's very true. You're correct, and I have no right to bring it up, much less to push it, so I'm sorry for that. However, I will ask that, while you're here, if something is wrong, … would you please do anything you can to help my babies?"

"No."

The finality was such that she stared at him in shock.

He shook his head. "I'll take what may be a very different stance than most people, and I will look after the mother."

"Why, … why would you do that?" The shock she felt was apparent on her face.

"You could have another baby," he replied, "but Bullard? He can't live without you." She stared at him, her bottom lip trembling, and he knew she was about to burst into tears. He sighed. "Look. That's not an easy thing for me to say, and that's why I'm trying to tell you to not even think about it. Obviously I would do everything I could to help, but, if a decision had to be made between one or the other, I know very well which way I would go. It's painful to hear it, and, if it's not something you're comfortable with, you need to get there," he stated. "I know that you will think I'm an absolute asshole for this, which is also why I was hoping to avoid the conversation."

She bit her lip, as she stared up at him. "There's really nothing I can say to you, is there?"

"No, there isn't, but you might have more luck with Lacy."

Surprised, she looked at him. "Why is that?"

"Because she's all heart. She would understand your wish to keep your child alive. She would side with that over Bullard."

"It's Bullard's baby too."

"It is, but Bullard needs you in a way that I've not really seen too many men need a partner," Bojan shared. "As I told you, you have another chance at having another baby, but only if you are alive."

"Do I though?" she asked sadly. "I'm not getting any younger."

He frowned at her. "Yes, you do."

Such an odd note filled his words that she turned suddenly, stared at him, and asked in apparent delight, "I'll have more?" He glared at her, and she threw up her hands. "Well, you can hardly get mad at me for asking."

He groaned. "See? This is why I don't like answering these questions."

"Fine," she muttered. "I'll talk to Lacy then. She did say that she would stay here that long at least."

"Good," he replied, then hesitated. "Look. If there's anything that we can do, we will. Just understand that we will come from very different places on this issue."

She sighed and nodded. "That's good to know, and at least I know where you stand."

"It's the same place I've always stood," he stated, "for

life, not for future life. You have the opportunity to have more children, but I can't guarantee that this one will be okay." Then he stopped and added with a shake of his head. "And I'm only talking about the one here because the other one's fine."

She nodded. "Right, and, for that, I'm very grateful."

"You should be, and that's another reason that you must survive. Just remember to be grateful, and everything else will fall into place."

"Do you think so?"

The way she posed it, she was obviously rather desperate for hope, and he hated it, absolutely hated it. Giving hope and then having it not work out was a tough nut to crack. "The trouble is, you want something from me, and, if I give you an answer now, and it turns out the opposite, it will be hard for you to forgive, and I don't want to be on the back side of that."

"Lacy mentioned something similar," Leia murmured. "I really won't do that. I'm just trying to keep my children alive."

He smiled. "I understand that, but these things are beyond our control. Sometimes miracles happen and sometimes? Not so much. Now I'm going back out to join the men before I have to explain to Bullard why I'm locked in a room with you."

She burst out laughing at that and said, "He would have absolutely no problem with my being in here."

"Yeah, says you," Bojan quipped, with a wry smile. "I'm here to tell you that it doesn't matter. You're still his wife. He still cares, and it'll still make a difference."

"Seriously?" She looked at him. "He's got no reason to be jealous."

"It's not even about jealousy. It's more … possessive-ness."

"Okay, I get it, and I'm not doing anything to try and trigger that in him because I know how much—"

"He really cares for you desperately," Bojan pointed out. "So we won't push it."

"Agreed." She glanced back at him before she walked out. She stopped at the door, "Thank you, Bojan."

He nodded. "Just remember. You may not be thanking me down the road."

"I will," she replied. "I do understand the sanctity of life, and I have certainly seen more than my fair share of death and times when things could or could not be done or when difficult choices had to be made. If you do what you can, it would still be an attempt with your best judgment of the situation, using the resources available at the moment. I can't ask for any more than that and will respect the effort, regardless of the outcome." And, with that, she walked out.

He left the room slowly, wondering if she really meant it because, in his experience, it wasn't necessarily that way. Women tended to blame people when things didn't go the way they wanted.

He could heal some things but not everything, and the aftermath could be too much to bear.

At the same time, he had known that when he'd opened the energy door to help Lacy, it would be a door he could no longer close. Damn it, he would if he could. He'd already tried, but it just wouldn't work anymore. He knew it, and she knew it. Now that he'd let her back into his life, he would also let her into his headspace, which was essentially letting her back into his heart. He had to wonder at the irony of that, when he'd worked so hard to keep her out. Now, here she was, in his heart once again, and it wasn't even her own fault. He couldn't blame her for it, and it was his own decision to help her. Yet how could he do any less? It was Lacy after all.

CHAPTER 6

W HEN LACY WOKE up, she felt that much better yet
again. She sat up and slowly got to her feet, then
gingerly walked to the bathroom. It was obvious she was still
struggling to heal, but what could she expect after being
shot? It would clearly take a bit longer than a quick nap, but,
at the same time, she felt better than before her nap. Yes, she
knew a lot of that was because of Bojan's initial assistance,
and she was delighted that he'd stepped up to help her out.

She knew he would be offended at the thought that he
wouldn't have done so, but, with him, there were no
guarantees. He was all about doing the right thing, but
sometimes doing the right thing didn't mean what you
thought it should.

He'd done the right thing once before for her, and it had
created a bond that neither one of them had expected or had
even wanted. She still felt as if she was constantly apologizing
for it because, if there was ever something she hadn't wanted
to do, locking a good man into something he didn't want
was right up there. The whole situation made her crazy.

She also knew that the rest of Bullard's group was incredibly curious and wanted explanations, but, in this case,
the explanation wasn't hers to give, though Bojan shouldn't
be pressured either. She knew that by helping with her pain,
he had exposed himself to even more scrutiny, yet he did it

anyway, and, for that, she was grateful.

After using the facilities, she washed her face and quickly stripped out of the hospital gown. She put on a very loose dress, checking her bandage. Knowing it would be checked constantly, regardless who might be coming and going in this group-oriented operation, she added a soft pair of shorts under the dress to make sure she would be appropriately covered, at least for the moment.

As she moved carefully down the stairs, she realized Bojan already knew where she was, when she heard a chair pushed back with the carelessness of someone in a hurry. As she expected, he appeared around the base of the stairway, glaring up at her. "Yes, I know," she said, stopping and glaring right back. "You would prefer that I stay in bed."

"Absolutely I would, and you know damn well that's where you belong."

Still holding her own, she maintained eye contact and replied, "I just wanted to come down and see if there was any news."

"No, you wanted to come down and act like you haven't been shot," he snapped. She glared at him again. "Hey, it's your funeral." He shrugged, then stepped out of her way.

Lacy asked him, "Did you ever stop to think about how much we could get done if we weren't always fighting?" He snorted at that, but she knew the others had heard. As she stepped into the dining room, nothing but curious gazes came from all sides of the room. She smiled at them. "Hey, I'm feeling much better. I know I'm not supposed to be up, but I'm just here for a little bit, just trying to feel normal. Then I promise I'll go back to bed."

Bullard glared at her. "How the hell are you even up and moving?" he asked.

She sighed. "Well, some of that precog that I mentioned can also be twisted into healing energy," she explained, with a sigh. "And, in that case, I can heal faster than most people, but I am definitely still injured, and it will still take some time to heal."

Bullard looked over at Bojan, shooting daggers. "Did you help her?"

"A little bit early on, yes. What else was I supposed to do? … Ignore her?" Bojan asked.

"No, of course not," Bullard muttered, bewildered and shaking his head. "We never understood Terkel, and to think that you two guys are the same is mind-boggling."

Bojan shook his head. "I don't think anybody is the same as Terkel," he argued. "Some things can't be explained, and Terkel is one of them."

"No, I get that," Bullard agreed, "but he's partly responsible for Leia and me being rescued. So whatever works, works. I just wish we could tap into it."

"Terkel would say that you can," Lacy piped up. "He would say that everybody has abilities."

"Of course he would," Bullard muttered, with a sigh. "That doesn't make it something that the rest of us can just turn around and create out of thin air though, especially with the talent of a log."

"I don't know about that, but I'm pretty sure you could try to do some things to begin to make it work for you, but again … I'm not the expert."

"Are you sure?" Bullard asked, with a piercing gaze in her direction.

She looked at him in surprise and then nodded. "Yeah, I've never ever taught this to anybody," she replied, with a shrug. "I mean, how could I, without opening a huge can of worms? It's hard to even explain to you guys, and you're all staring at me as if I have the answers to the universe. And I don't. Believe me. … And nothing you can pry out of me will make it any easier. I know a certain amount of energy is around us, and I treat it like a soft ball. … I toss it and kick it around, as need be. In this case, I also use it to heal this …" She pointed to her wound. "We all have the ability to heal. We all have the ability to do lots of things," she stated calmly. "However, just because I can tell you to do that much … doesn't mean you will turn around and start kicking around soft balls of healing energy."

At that, Ryland started to laugh. "No, but, man, the picture in my head of everybody outside practicing such a skill is pretty amazing to even consider. Seriously, that's how you view it?"

"It's something that I've done since I was child. I treated the energy almost like a game, as a part of me. And maybe because of that, it ended up being such a part of me and a part of my world. I don't really know, but I've been hoping to talk to Terkel about it one day and to see if there's any way to develop it further than what I currently have. I went to med school to try and help people, so that leaves me without too many options for the time being."

"He'll take you on in an instant. You know that," Bullard stated. "Anybody with that kind of talent, Terkel wants and helps develop it further."

"Sometimes I wonder about bringing it up, but I don't really know the man," she admitted in an anguished tone. "We've touched base on the odd occasion, but it's not as if I'm in his sphere or anything," she said, for lack of a better word.

"Yeah, you are," Bojan disagreed. "You always knock

yourself down."

She looked astonished at hearing him say that. "Yeah? It's not so much that I knock myself down," she replied in exasperation. "I just don't build myself up."

"And there is a difference, isn't there?" Leia pointed out.

Just then, Pia walked in, pushing a cart laden with food.

Lacy looked at it and smiled. "So, do I get to stay and eat?"

Pia looked at her, as if noticing her the first time, and his mouth dropped in shock. "Why are you even out of bed?" he roared.

She groaned. "Oh, I'll take that as a no then."

"I suggest you eat," Leia noted, "and then get back to bed for some rest, before they decide to argue further, which they will."

"Well, that was the plan," Lacy shared, with a sigh. "I just hadn't really expected to be surrounded by all these mother hens around here."

"You were shot today," Bullard pointed out. "You might want to remember that in terms of everybody else's expectations."

"Oh." She frowned, looking at them. "Was that today?" They all frowned at her and nodded. "Well, it's a good thing that I wasn't badly hurt and that I had the benefit of immediate care by such a highly skilled surgical team," she said, with a bright cheerful smile. She maneuvered herself to the table, then dropped in the chair beside Bojan.

He looked at her, raised an eyebrow, and declared, "Don't be looking to me for protection when they all come charging to get your ass back up to bed, because I'll be helping them."

She glared at him and added, "You know perfectly well

how I'm doing."

"I know somewhat how you're doing," Bojan replied, "but, in order to know more than that, I would have to look deeper, and I'm not doing that."

"Too late," she snapped. "You already opened the damn door."

At that, he glared at her, then got up and walked around to the far end of the table and sat down, basically as far away from her as he could get. It was hard to handle the hurt his actions brought out, even though they both knew why he was doing it, but that still didn't make it any easier.

Feeling her bottom lip start to tremble, she firmed herself up, then looked over at Pia and said, "I didn't want to make you do the stairs, so I came down for a little bit of food, if that's all right." Her tone was very formal. "I promise I'll go right back to bed."

He just looked at her, dumbfounded, then over at Bojan, who remained silent. Pia didn't say anything but started serving the food, giving her a platter first. She took that to mean she was supposed to eat and then to leave. She ate quietly, the conversation around her uncomfortable and muted, yet it flowed nonetheless.

By the time she had eaten, she felt a little better. However, at the same time, Bojan's actions hurt her way more than any bullet. She finished eating, then stood and nodded to the rest of the table. "If you'll excuse me, I'll be going back up." Carefully she headed toward the stairway. She made it to the second step before the first strangled sob broke free. Behind her, Bojan swore, and seconds later he picked her up and carried her up the stairs.

"Leave me alone," she sobbed. "I know how much you hate me. Just leave me alone. I'll be fine."

"Shut up," he said, his voice not unkind. "You know I can't stand a woman's tears."

"Yeah, but what you really mean is you can't stand me."

He sighed. "Lacy, if that were true, I'd be gone. You know that. I don't have to be or to do anything other than what I want."

"No, of course not. You're always just you, an arrogant, mean, and pompous ass," she said, for lack of a better word. Tears streamed down her cheeks, even as he pushed open the door to her bedroom, carried her in, then gently laid her down on the bed.

"I'm not trying to be, you know."

"You don't have to *try*," she muttered, feeling the pain kick in something awful. "You just do it naturally."

"Well, sorry about that," he said. "Some things take a little longer."

"They don't have to," she argued. "You just enjoy keeping it alive."

At that, he stopped and stared at her, his face twisting. "Is that what you think?"

She continued to glare at him. "I'm in my bed, so you can leave now."

He hesitated, then nodded. "That's probably for the best."

"For the best, of course it is. What else could you possibly want with me? You've already humiliated me, yet, at the same time, I'm supposed to thank you for keeping me alive."

"I don't want you to thank me," he said, then stepped back, frowning at her.

She tried hard to return the frown, but she wasn't feeling well enough to manage it. She waved at the door. "Go back down and eat," she ordered.

"Stop ordering me around," he said, with a sigh.

"That's hardly the worst thing in the world," she muttered. "No, wait, apparently that's me. I'm the worst thing in the world. So leave, go on, get out of here."

"You're telling me to leave?" he asked, with a note of astonishment.

"Yes, I know you don't want to be here."

He sighed. "I wanted an awful lot of things in my world that I didn't get a chance to have," he reminded her, "but you still don't get to order me around."

She sniffed, pointed at the door. "Hell if I care, now go."

Shaking his head, he walked to the door, then turned back. "Now would you please stay up here, take care of yourself, and don't get into trouble?"

"That's all I do, right? Get into trouble. That's me," she muttered.

"Yeah, I know," he said, "and honestly you're killing me."

At that, he stepped back to leave, and she couldn't hold back the tears any longer. She rolled over and sobbed into her pillow. Then hearing a strangled exclamation, she suddenly felt herself gently picked up in his arms and tucked against his chest. He wrapped another blanket around her.

"Stop, please, stop," he whispered, but she couldn't.

Lacy was well past the point of no return. She cried and cried. When she finally ran out of tears, she fell into a deep slumber, not even realizing that she was still wrapped up in his arms, all the while she bawled her heart out.

When she woke again, she felt better, but raw, as if the inside of her had been ripped out. And she was still wrapped up in his arms. When she blinked up at him, he looked down at her, letting loose a hard sigh.

"What am I to do with you?" Then he lowered his head and kissed her.

It opened a well in her heart that she'd been trying so damn hard to keep shut, but now there was absolutely no way to resist, especially in the state she was in. She struggled with the blanket and finally got her arms free, then wrapped them around his neck and held on tight.

When he finally lifted his head, he rested his forehead against hers. "Jesus," he muttered.

She didn't say anything, her throat sore, her heart beating too hard, too fast, at something she'd wanted for far too long. She just waited, knowing that his next words would either crush her or set her free—could completely destroy her world.

He lifted his head, looked down at her, and sadness filled his eyes. "I'm sorry. I've been an absolute ass."

She raised one eyebrow, scarcely able to breathe, scared what his next words would be.

THIS WAS THE part that Bojan had held off from forever, and suddenly, not only was he here, he was on the other side of it. He crushed her up against his chest, immediately releasing her when he heard her gasp in pain. "I'm so sorry," he whispered.

She shook her head. "I'm fine. I am, really." He glared down at her, and she smiled. "You know I am."

He nodded slowly. "It took me a long time to forgive you. You know that, right?"

"I didn't think you ever had."

He nodded almost absentmindedly at that. "No, maybe

not. It wasn't exactly what I'd planned on doing, but I did."

"Well, none of this is what I'd ever planned on either."

"I guess I hadn't been ready to acknowledge that," he admitted. "For some reason, it was easier to blame you than to see that our actions back then changed the path of my life. It set me onto something I wasn't planning but absolutely wanted to be on, then suddenly it wasn't my path anymore," he shared. "It was pretty devastating."

"Yeah, I got that," she said. "You made that very clear."

He winced at that. "I wasn't trying to be cruel."

"No, but you didn't even have to try," she replied, some of her own anger and heartache rising. "It seemed to come to you quite naturally."

"I think, when we're hurting, we strike out, not necessarily realizing how much we're hurting the other person. So, for the record, I don't blame you."

She stared up at him. "You don't? Seriously?"

"No, I don't," he confirmed, "and I realize it's taken me way too long to get there."

She nodded. "Yeah, it sure has."

He quirked his lips at her. "Not going to let me off the hook, are you?"

She shrugged. "All these years have been pretty rough."

He sighed. "No, I get it, on both sides."

She nodded. "And, for what it's worth, I'm sorry. If I'd had any idea—"

"No, and that's the part I had to figure out, finally realizing that, as much as I wanted to make you the bad guy in this, you weren't the bad guy, and you weren't the one responsible. Plus I had always looked at you as a little sister, and our actions didn't measure up to what a good sister or a good brother should be doing," he added. "The guilt has really been something I've struggled with."

She snorted at that. "That's hardly the issue, but I can see that, for you, with all that bloody honor, … it choked you up."

"Not exactly choking me up, when I couldn't even be civil to you." He gently hugged her close again. "But, with you taking that damn bullet," he muttered, looking down at her side, "I didn't even hesitate."

"Good, I'm glad. It would have been a much different story if you hadn't started the healing process ahead of time."

"Maybe, but that's not what I want to do in life."

"Oh, I'm very aware of that," she noted, giving him half a smile, "and I get it. I know it sounds like I don't really understand—and I never meant to make life as difficult for you as it probably appears that I did—but honestly it was necessary at the time."

"Yeah, it was," he agreed, "very necessary for the person in question."

"For the child in question," she pointed out.

He nodded. "That part is water under the bridge. However, the ramifications in my world were another story." He had to leave it at that.

She nodded. "There's not much I can say except to reiterate I didn't do it on purpose and had no idea what the repercussion would be. Still, they'd been massive and you paid the ultimate price, not me." She tried for a calm deep breath. "For the record," she murmured, "I really am sorry."

He sighed. "We won't go there. Remember?"

"Well, I think it would help if we would clear the air. I know there are an awful lot of questions downstairs, and we will get hit with it one way or another. They have to ask questions."

"Particularly of me, since I haven't done very well by you." When she looked at him in surprise, he shrugged. "Not too many men would appreciate anybody treating a woman the way I treated you."

"You mean, by saving my life?" she asked.

"No, of course not," he said, with a sigh. "You always make things so simple, and you know that it's not that simple at all."

"It always was for me," she murmured. "At least I thought so."

"Yeah, and that's what got us into trouble," he stated. "So, we will give them an explanation, but I really didn't want to air our dirty laundry here."

"If we could have maintained some degree of civility, we might have successfully done that, but I think we're well past that."

"Yeah, and, for that, I owe them an explanation, and I owe you an apology. It was never my intention to humiliate you."

She looked up at him and smiled. "Believe me. I know that."

He groaned. "Doesn't matter. I still feel that I'm very much in the wrong, and that's not a position I particularly care to be in."

She chuckled. "I don't think anybody does, and I'm sorry that you feel you need to do something about it, that you feel the need to explain. I think they would all understand."

"I don't," he replied. "You found people here who care about you."

"Yeah? What a surprise," she quipped, with a weak smile. "It took me a long time to find acceptance within myself. I felt terribly guilty for the longest time."

"And, for that, I can apologize. Then you can apologize, and we can still end up not getting anywhere," he said, "or we can just move on and acknowledge that it happened, knowing that we will have to provide some sort of an explanation for everybody downstairs to calm down the atmosphere here. Then hopefully we can get past it."

"So, how do you want to do it?"

He frowned. "It's probably best to just take it on the chin. I'll go down and explain what happened and tell them that things will be easier between us now."

"Well, you're not doing it alone."

"Really, and why not?"

"Because it's my fault."

"No," he declared. "The time for that kind of blame is well past."

"But you can't just take the blame for something that I started."

He stared at her with a wry expression. "We will discuss that at another time because, at the moment, I don't think *who is to blame* is really part of it, as much as just making peace with the people downstairs. Especially since we are guests in their house."

"I know"—Lacy winced—"not to mention how badly I've already blown things with Leia."

"Do you really see her being in trouble?" he asked.

"I don't know what I see," she admitted, sounding vexed. "Just so much is going on, and I don't know how much of that is because you are here."

"Maybe—with a little bit of work—the two of us can clear up our issues, and then we can help them get Leia through this."

"It would be nice if we could," Lacy agreed, "because

I'm not sure that Leia will have more children."

"Yet I'm pretty sure that's already in the plans," he mumbled, staring off in the distance.

"Well, I thought that too, but I feel that this soul of the ghost twin is important. He or she needs to stay with them."

"Great, so we will do everything we can to help her. You do know healing everybody isn't how I want to spend my life, right?"

"I know," she noted. "Which is one of the reasons I'm trying to spend my life saving people, when I can, … so that you're off the hook, you know?"

"I don't think it works that way."

"I'm not sure we have a choice anyway." She shifted so that she was out from under the blanket. "I suggest we go down and clear things up. Then maybe at least we can get some sleep tonight."

"Maybe," he murmured, "will you be okay to get up?" He looked at her with concern, as she walked to the bathroom.

"I'm feeling better. I'm just not great, you know?"

"I don't really want to take away more pain," he explained cautiously, looking at her for understanding.

"I get that," she replied, "and I agree that it's better if I don't do too much. It's just a hardship that will take some getting used to, and the fact that I know that I could be pain free doesn't help. Yet I know this is the best thing for me."

He nodded slowly, watching her move gingerly as she came back out of the bathroom.

"Come on, then," Lacy said. "Let's go face the music together."

"It's *my* music," Bojan stated. "You should just stay here and relax."

"Not happening," she declared. "It will be more expedient if we show a united front."

He sighed. "You're awfully amiable, considering how things all blew up back then, plus all that's happening now," he pointed out.

"I was devastated at the time, and torn, but I didn't know how to make it right, couldn't figure out a way to get there."

"That's because there is no *making it right*," he muttered. "I just hadn't yet come to the point where I understood that it wasn't you who was in the wrong."

"I'm just glad we're finally talking and getting somewhere now."

"Come on then. Let's go downstairs and talk to them." And, with that, he walked to the door and watched her critically as she carefully walked over.

"I'm fine," she murmured. "At least you've given me another shot of energy to get through this, so thanks for that."

He shrugged self-consciously. "I figure this stress won't go away if we don't clear the air, and you probably won't heal with that stress all around you, so the best thing is for me to go down and face it head-on."

"No, we're both going," she reiterated.

He looked at her and smiled. "It's always been that way with you, hasn't it? Black was white, white was black."

"Ha, that's just your version," she muttered.

Bojan watched her closely as she went down the stairs. Everybody was still at the dinner table, as Pia was serving dessert. Bojan and Lacy walked in, his arm firmly around her. One by one, everybody looked up, with varying expressions.

With a sigh, Bojan faced them all and stated, "You guys are entitled to an explanation."

"YOU DON'T OWE us anything," Leia replied, "but it would help us to understand what's going on between you two. The undercurrents have made it difficult for us to know if we can do anything to help."

"No, there's nothing you can do to help, Leia, but thank you," Bojan replied. "We decided that the best thing we could do—now that we've sorted out our differences, to the extent that we can at the moment—is to give you a bit of an explanation. But, if that whiskey is still on the table, I could use a little of it." He looked at Pia.

Pia walked to the sidebar, poured him a shot, and brought it over, along with two slices of cheesecake. Bojan looked down at the combo and smiled. "That should help."

With that, and Lacy sitting at his side, Bojan looked around at them and began, "Lacy was raised in my family, as a foster sister. She was always the little sister, the one I looked out for, the one who always got into trouble, yet somehow always managed to get out of it. We never discussed our abilities, and I never knew she had any. I was still struggling with whatever mine were. Don't even bother to ask me to explain what they are because they always evolve, to the point that I don't always know myself." He stopped for a moment and took a shaky breath to collect his thoughts.

"We were raised in a very dysfunctional family, with a lot of fighting, a lot of infidelity on both sides, a lot of betrayals, a lot of sadness," he explained. "Yet, at one point in time, I found Michelle, the love of my life, and everything was perfect. We were engaged to be married. She was pregnant with my child. She was my everything," he revealed. "I had stopped by the house to collect more of my things, since I was getting married the following week. Because of all the family problems, I knew that Lacy was trying to get out of the house as well, just because life was so horrible and chaotic there.

"Anyway, the neighbor had come over, screaming for help because her baby was in trouble. We both ran over in order to help her, and the little girl was definitely not breathing. It looked like she was dying, choking maybe. I didn't even know, but Lacy dove in to try and help, using her healing abilities that I didn't really understand or didn't even know that she had at the time. However, her energy wasn't enough, so she grabbed me and my energy to help.

"Now, whether I had my own energy powers before this point in time or not, I don't know. Yet somehow Lacy knew, instinctively knew that the only way to save the little girl was for us to bond. It took quite a bit out of both of us, but we saved the little girl, which was amazing, and there were smiles all around.

"The problem with the methodology that Lacy used came from the bonding," he stressed. "Because Lacy and I were then bonded, my fiancée, the mother of my child, was no longer somebody I could bond with."

Shocked gasps came from around the table, and Lacy reached out a hand and gripped his.

Bojan stared down at it, a sad smile on his face. "So, I'm sure you guys can understand that the ensuing days, weeks, and months even were traumatic and difficult. I never did get married because I knew, from that moment on, that I could never love her because of this bond that existed between Lacy and me. As you might imagine, it was an awful and confusing time. I absolutely hated Lacy for what she'd done to my life. My upcoming marriage, my child, my girlfriend, my life, it was all turned upside down. Then …" He stopped, his jaw working for a moment, before Lacy reached across and gave him a hug, then turned to the rest.

"His fiancée committed suicide, with his unborn baby," she whispered. "So, with that single act, … with that choice I made while trying to save that neighbor child, I cost him everything."

Absolute silence filled the room, as everybody digested what they had just heard.

Finally Bojan continued. "So, there are a couple of things to understand about this. One, Lacy didn't know that the bonding would happen, but I blamed her anyway. My fiancée blamed Lacy as well and ultimately took her own life. It was a terrible scene, similar to when Lacy and I had fought together to save the neighbor's little girl, except we were fighting to save my child. We were in a raw, ugly panic, where we felt that the soul wasn't strongly attached, and, in the ensuing fight to save Michelle, we lost the child."

Shock settled over the table, as everyone imagined what that scene must have been like. They were all very still, looking between Bojan and Lacy. "Michelle died at the same time, her pregnancy at thirty-two weeks."

At that, Leia paled, her hands going to her belly.

"The baby would have been viable, had we had any way to save her," Bojan added. "Afterward, … after I buried my family, I directed my fury at Lacy and my biological family and anybody else who had the misfortune to get close enough to me. Then I went into the military, and, like many of you, I became a skilled hunter, a killer, more or less. I did my time in the military, then went private, and thankfully didn't join the bad guys but stayed on the side of right. I have funneled a lot of negative energy toward Lacy because of everything that happened," he admitted. "Only when I saw her shot and hurting did I step out of that bubble of self-pity. Without a thought, I bent down and used the same energy, knowing full well that doing so would open a door I had slammed shut in her face long ago.

"She is not to blame for any of that, although she will say she is. But she's not. She had no idea that pulling me in to help her the way she did would bond us in that way. She was just trying to save a little girl, and I was right there with her. So, I totally get it if you guys want me to leave or if you have a hard time with this. I'm really not into oversharing, and, as far as I'm concerned, this subject is closed. It's been enough of a shit storm all around."

And again came silence.

At that, Lacy looked over at the others. "It's partly why we know about Leia's baby. It's also partly why we each have some abilities we're unsure about. In bonding, we seem to have created an unstable relationship."

"How does that work?" Ryland asked, confused.

"From what I've formulated, because we share energy and are bonded, as I have developed my abilities, it has left him a certain amount of development space that's available but unused." She gave him a sideways look. "And, as he has developed skills, that has left space for me to develop. … That has left us both unsure because what is natural for me to develop won't necessarily be comfortable for him, and some of his natural skills are not what I would think to try. I'm sure Terkel would have a heyday if he ever got us long enough to do some testing, though maybe that's something we should look at in order to become whole again," she suggested. "It's definitely been a very tumultuous time for us."

And again came more silence.

Bullard looked from Lacy to Bojan to his men, then back again, and whispered, "What the hell? For people like us, who don't even know anything about this, to even think something like that is possible seems crazy."

"That's part of the problem," Bojan agreed. "We didn't know either. I didn't know it was possible. I didn't know any of that, and neither did she. Again, it was that desperate attempt to try and save a neighbor's child."

"And because of that, there can never be somebody to blame," Leia noted. "We've all had various events in our lives where we tried to save somebody, and all of us have also taken part in some of them where it just wasn't possible." She faced Bojan. "I am so sorry for Michelle and what she went through."

At that, an audible sob was heard, and everybody turned to look at Lacy, as she bit her lip and nodded. "There was nothing I could say to her that made a difference. I tried time and time again, but I just couldn't do anything to make it right," she shared. "I really tried. However, short of dying myself, I could do nothing for her, and believe me. I did consider that as well."

She whispered, "You have no idea what *tumultuous* means until somebody you're bonded with wants nothing to do with you, and then you watch his partner and child die in his arms." Lacy shook her head. "So I know this is difficult to understand and to accept, but, if you are tempted to judge us, please don't. It's been done already, ... mostly by us.

We've both been to hell and back. I don't know how or why we both ended up here at the same time. All I know is that I put out the concern that I was worried about Leia, and somehow you guys brought Bojan back into my world, though I'm not sure he's ready to thank you for that part either." She gave them half a smile.

Bullard still stared at her in shock. Then he looked around at the others and announced, "I'm not sure blame needs to be assigned in any case. Having a child of my own right now, the thought of watching him or her die? Well, it would kill me. And Leia? I can't even think about it. But then to know it was due to the action of somebody else?" Bullard whistled. "I am not sure I'd forgive you either."

The silence that followed spoke volumes.

"I know that," Lacy whispered in tears.

"Honestly I would like to think that I'm a good man and that I know right from wrong," Bullard added, "but this would be one of those instances where right from wrong would get very confusing. So, I certainly don't blame you or Bojan. I don't think anybody needs to blame either of you. Clearly you two have blamed yourselves more than enough."

Everybody turned to look at Bojan and Lacy.

Lacy sighed and shared a look with Bojan.

Bojan nodded. "The fact is, there is no blame that anybody could lob in my direction that I haven't already charged myself with ten times over and more. Michelle was twenty-nine years old, and we had the most brilliant future ahead of us. The two of us together, we would have been great, and, to this day, I still mourn that loss. I don't know how one couldn't," he said, with a shrug.

"We were set to have a family and a bright future, and it was gone just like that. But, as I have finally come to realize,

I need to move on, and I have to do it in a way that makes sense for the world I'm in, which is not in any way clear, concise, or understandable. One of the things that never made sense to me was just how confusing all of this energy work could be. I mean, if this is supposed to be correct and right and a done deal, then it should be a done deal that makes sense. Yet I'm not there. I am moving in that direction, however. Having Lacy get shot like that and having to open myself up to helping her to heal? ... Well, that also opened the doorway between the two of us again that I had slammed shut."

There was a shocked murmur around the table.

"Whether I like it or not, that bond between us is now open and flowing once again, and where we go with it from there? I have no idea. I also don't know whether putting it all out there to you will make things better or worse, but we felt the only way forward was to be honest about it. That way, Leia and Lacy have less stress and can focus on healing."

CHAPTER 7

L ACY WOKE UP the next morning, with a smile on her face. Last night she and Bojan had both quickly excused themselves, knowing that the group needed to discuss the bomb that they had just dropped on them. For most people, to even know such a thing was possible was just horrifying. These people were all in very strong and intensely committed relationships, so to think of that being ripped apart would cause many of them to stop in their tracks.

She had left Bojan at her bedroom door last night, firmly closing it in his face. Then she went and had a shower, standing there and crying for what seemed like hours. For the loss of his fiancée and child, for the loss of his future, for the years that Lacy and Bojan had been apart, and for all the hours, days, weeks, and months that she had been torment- ed, knowing that, for her, there could never be anyone else. Seeing what happened to Bojan and Michelle and their child was wrong and had been too much to handle. Lacy's years of anguish, so hard and at the front of her mind, were like a needle in her side, and now that the dam had broken, she felt beyond exhausted. Still not knowing what her new world even looked like, she crashed into bed. ... With her hair damp and her body barely dried off, she crawled under the single sheet and collapsed into an endless night.

But now it was morning, and she didn't have a specific

psychic feeling as to how anything might be. She slowly sat up and walked to the bathroom, and things seemed lighter, easier somehow. She moved with more fluidity, as if everything that had pulled her down, everything that had been a weight on her joints, on her shoulders, was gone.

When she finished with her morning rituals, she looked at the relatively small selection of clothes she'd brought with her and put on another sundress, then slipped into her sandals and walked slowly downstairs, hesitant as to what kind of reception she would get.

As she walked into the kitchen, the kitchen itself was empty and so was the adjoining dining room. She stared at the pool and wondered if she should have gone for a swim first. Though it would have been against medical advice, she was certain it would have made her feel a lot better. Yet she didn't feel bad, just a bit numb somehow, and, painwise, that was fine by her.

She poured herself a cup of coffee just as Pia walked in. When he stopped and stared at her, she gave him a tentative smile, lifted her cup, and said, "Hope you don't mind?"

He shook his head, his face softening. "Of course not. I thought you would be in the pool. And, so you know, Bullard has the place on lockdown, extra guards on the perimeter, while we work on enhancing the technological aspects of our system." He sighed. "You are safe by the pool again."

Lacy smiled. "Thanks. … Not sure my wound should be in the pool just yet. I'll have this coffee and see." She stepped outside, deliberately not looking at the doorway where she had been shot. She walked over to find a seat in the shadows, yet that didn't feel right either. So, within thirty seconds, she got up and moved to the sunny spot, wondering if maybe now she could step out and live a normal life, instead of one that held secrets and heartache.

She sat here with her face to the sun, sipping her coffee, trying to let the new day sink in.

"How are you feeling this morning?" Leia asked, as she made her way over and sat down beside her. She looked at her friend with a wry smile.

"Better in many ways," Lacy replied. "I'm sorry for all that you guys had to endure last night. Obviously we would have preferred to keep everything personal and private, not have our world broken apart and exposed like that."

Leia shook her head. "We didn't understand what was going on though, so that gave us an explanation, far more than any of us would have thought was possible. Believe me. Nobody is judging you or Bojan today," she stated, "not that anybody was yesterday either. However, after hearing what happened, I think we're all just grateful it wasn't us."

That startled a laugh out of Lacy, and she nodded, her smile wide. "Isn't that the truth? Believe me. I wish it'd been somebody else too."

Leia grinned at her. "Sorry, I was trying to put you at ease. Really though, I think it was a good decision to clear the air. So, now that you and Bojan are …"

"Honestly, I don't know what Bojan and I are," Lacy interrupted, looking over at Leia. "I know that we're bonded, and that'll never change. I don't see any way that it ever could, but I'm also not sure that we are 100 percent together either. Let's just say we're on the pathway."

At that, Leia beamed. "I think that is exactly where you need to be. It's now a whole new day for both of you, a day of exploration, I guess," she noted, with a smile. "So, I, for one, am delighted." Then she studied Lacy critically. "Pia even mentioned it, and I agree. You do seem to be moving easily."

"Well, I've been sitting here for the last five minutes, so not much moving going on."

"No, I saw you come out though," Leia explained. "I was in the garden, pulling weeds."

Looking at Leia's massive girth, Lacy shook her head. "Of course you were."

Leia laughed. "Hey, it helps me to stop worrying about my babies."

"Ah," Lacy murmured, "but, yes, I am feeling better. I had a shower and didn't even really notice the pain. I took off the bandage."

Leia stared. "You're kidding?"

Lacy shrugged. "Just like other things in my world of healing, the healing of my physical body can speed up as well."

"Good Lord," Leia muttered under her breath. "I would like to have a look at that wound."

Lacy nodded. "Okay. Remember, it's not something I can teach you to do or somehow give you. It's just what I can do myself, and, beyond that, I don't know."

"Well, we will all try to learn," Leia stated. "The fact that you're here and that you have the ability to help heal others ... is why I'm hoping you will stay, at least through the birth."

"I do have classes and exams to take, but, since my practicum happens to be with you, of course I'll be here."

"I'm hoping you'll come back for a second practicum as well," Leia added. "I know you'll have to be at university for a couple months, but ..."

"It's six weeks, I think," Lacy corrected. "And you will

have motherhood fully upon you at that point in time, so I doubt you will be doing surgeries for a while."

"No, I'll need to take a few months off," Leia agreed, "but Bullard is here, and I can always assist in the clinic, if need be. But, if you were here," she explained, looking at Lacy intently, "we could continue the practice, until I'm back up and working."

"To a certain extent, yes," she murmured. "I'm also heading over to Terkel's place in a few months, so I'm not sure what that will look like either."

Leia tilted her head slightly to the side. "Why?"

Lacy looked at her friend and mentor. "Because a lot of babies are coming over there. And one thing I can do— particularly with people of energy—is help boost the healing energy all around."

"Ah." Leia nodded. "That's a good point. Here, there's only one of me."

"And over there, literally eight of them," Lacy shared.

At that, Leia's eyes widened. "Are they all pregnant?"

Lacy flashed her a bright grin. "They are, and some are having multiples."

"Good God," Leia said, "Terkel will have his hands full."

"I believe a nursery and a daycare center are now in the plans, as well as nannies and any number of other staff who might need to be brought on board," Lacy shared. "I'm just getting bits and pieces from Terkel." At that, she winced, as Terkel slipped into her brain.

Very true. If you're needed there though …

Leia reached across to squeeze Lacy's hand and asked, "What's the matter?"

"Terkel was just in my brain," Lacy said. "He's telling me that it's okay to stay here, if I'm needed. But, looking at the time frame, I need to be back there at a certain point too," she explained. She looked over at Leia. "You're likely to deliver early."

Leia nodded. "I would like to make thirty-six weeks in order to have both babies be *viable*," she noted, saying the word with emphasis.

"Agreed." At that, Lacy stiffened ever-so-slightly and then relaxed.

Leia looked at her, one eyebrow raised, as if to ask if anything were wrong.

Lacy shrugged. "Bojan walked into the kitchen. That's one of the things about being bonded. ... It enhances all our senses. We are very alert to the presence of the other."

"Interesting," Leia murmured. "I hate to say it, but what if something happens to one of you?"

"The bond can still exist, and I don't know if it can ever be broken," she replied. "That was one of the things we explored in the past, so he could be with Michelle," she murmured.

Just then the door banged open, and Bojan stepped out of the kitchen, holding a cup of coffee in his hand. He looked over at the ladies, then walked over to join them, his gaze assessing.

Lacy smiled up at him. "I'm fine."

He didn't say anything, just gave a curt nod, then turned toward Leia, his gaze still assessing.

Leia laughed. "I'm fine too."

"Good," he stated. "In that case you won't mind if I go for a swim." Already wearing swim shorts, he put the hot coffee down on the edge of the pool. Heading to the diving board, he executed the perfect dive and proceeded to do several laps.

"I should have done that myself," Lacy mumbled, "but I was feeling a little on the fragile side this morning."

"Yeah, no wonder," Leia murmured. "And thank you for sharing about this bond you have with Bojan. It did help to clear up a lot of issues."

"Yeah, I know."

"Do other people know?"

"Terkel knows. As do a couple of people on Terk's team. They were aware of Michelle's passing at the time, since we pulled in everyone we could to try and save the baby," she replied, brushing back the tears in her eyes.

Leia winced. "And is that an option if I have trouble? Can we pull in Terkel and some of his healers?"

"Yes, of course," Lacy confirmed, with a wide smile. "And, no, I wouldn't even give him a choice. I'll just drag him right into it." She laughed, while mentally sending Terkel a message at the same time. Then she continued her discussion with Leia. "I know Terk and his team won't have a problem helping, but again not everything is within our abilities."

"No, of course not," Leia admitted. "As a surgeon, I see that every day."

At that, Lacy winced. "You could try lying down instead of being out there, bent over on your hands and knees, gardening."

"But the thing about being on your hands and knees when you're pregnant," Leia clarified, "is that it feels so good to take the weight off your back."

At that, several other people walked out, Bullard among them. He walked over, wrapped an arm around Leia, kissed her on the top of the head, and murmured, "I'm surprised to find you out in the sun."

"It's not that hot this morning," she said, "but I do think it is time to go rest for a bit."

Lacy looked at her phone and was surprised to see it was already past ten in the morning. "Wow," she murmured. "I really slept in, didn't I?"

"You are injured," Bullard stated, his gaze piercing. "Although, to be honest, you don't really look it."

"I definitely still have a scar, but it's closed," she noted, nodding at him.

"I want to see that," Leia repeated.

"Okay, I'll walk in with you, and then you need to lie down." Lacy trooped in behind the two of them, as she headed to the surgery suite. Once there, she laid down on the exam table, pulling up her dress, so they could take a look at the wound. The look on their faces made her chuckle. "I gather there's not a whole lot to see."

"There's a bit of a scar and some redness around it," Bullard said, his fingers moving over her skin.

Lacy shifted onto her side, so they could take a look at the exit wound too.

"That's amazing," he murmured. "Now if we could just bottle you up and sell you to everybody else, we would never have to work again."

Leia laughed. "You don't have to work again anyway," she muttered, "and, if we *could* bottle Lacy up and split her into a million pieces, I would *give* the pieces away," she declared.

Bullard leaned over and kissed her on the lips this time. "You've got to give an entrepreneurial mind his moment of thinking just what that would do for us," he said, chuckling. "But to think that we could eradicate illness, injuries, with something like this? ... It is absolutely phenomenal." He looked over at Lacy. "That healing power you have is absolutely nuts."

She pulled down her dress, sat up, and nodded. "In this case it was also a minor injury, and, while you're giving me all the credit, remember that Bojan had a large part in that."

"Yeah, to think there's two of you is mind-boggling." Bullard frowned.

"More than a few," she corrected. "Terkel can be a hell of a healer, and he has quite a few incredible healers I've yet to meet on his team. I know one in particular who can do way more than I can."

Bullard just stared at her, stunned. He looked over at Leia, and his mouth opened, but Leia placed a finger against his lips. "I've already asked."

He nodded. "Of course you have." He sighed. "It's just that the next month will be a bit edgy."

"Understood," Lacy noted, as she hopped off the table, wincing ever-so-slightly at the motion, then walked to the door. "Now you need to rest, Leia."

"You sure I'll be early now, right?" Leia asked Lacy.

"You will be earlier, but I'm not sure how much." She hesitated at the door and then added, "Look. I'll talk to Bojan when I get a chance and when the time is *right*." She emphasized that last word because they all knew how delicate this situation was for all of them right now. "However, together Bojan and I are much stronger. That's one of the other aspects. Once the doors are open, … the potential for healing becomes that much more."

"Good Lord," Bullard declared. "Now I'm thinking I'll need one of you guys on staff on a permanent basis."

"Most of the time it's not even needed," Lacy pointed out, "and I don't know for sure, but I think Bojan is looking at potentially working with Terkel."

"Of course. We called Terkel looking for extra help, and he sent us Bojan."

"I think Terkel's probably the person to handle most of us," Lacy admitted, with a laugh. "And this energy work can entail all kinds of things." She hesitated a bit, after saying this.

"What?" Bullard asked. "Don't tell me that you've got more bombshells."

"Yeah, well," she replied, with a shrug. "We don't always have to be on the spot."

"What do you mean?" he asked, his gaze narrowed at her. "You mean, if you were in England at Terk's compound, you could still help?"

"Absolutely," she declared.

"Does it make a difference? The distance?" he asked.

"In some cases—although some people can do it with no notable difference at all—I guess it depends on what other tricks and tips I can learn from Terkel and his gang." Lacy smiled at the thought. "Still, as you're already *in* with Terkel himself, I don't think you will need to worry about having to ask for help when it's needed. Chances are, we'll already know ahead of time." And, with that, she turned and walked out, leaving the two of them in the surgery suite alone.

Lacy went up to her room and quickly changed into a bikini, knowing that the group would be buzzing over her speedy superior healing, then headed to the pool. As she got there, Bojan stood at the edge of the pool, sipping his coffee.

He looked up, his gaze going straight to her bullet wound. Then he just nodded without saying a word.

She dove in from the side and proceeded to do laps—comfortable, peaceful, reassuring physical laps—pulling her body back into alignment from the injury she had gone through. When she finished, she pulled herself out and sat on the side of the pool beside him.

"How does it feel?" he asked.

"Better," she said, with a nod. "Of course the two of us work better when we're together."

"Yeah, that's something we will have to keep in mind for Leia."

"I know," she agreed. "I did mention to her that we work stronger together, but that I would need to talk to you about it."

He nodded. "Obviously, when we're here, that will be part of it," he noted. "How did you sleep?"

"Like the dead," she replied bluntly. "I had a hell of a cry in the shower and then collapsed into bed. This morning it still feels different, new, odd, unique. I don't know. I'm getting there. How about you?"

"Same," he replied, always the man of few words.

She nodded. "I should have brought another cup of coffee out," she noted, yawning.

"Seems you need to go back to bed." He looked over at her, frowning.

"I'm fine. Just did a bit of exercise, but I didn't want to overdo it."

"Good call." He pulled himself up easily and asked, "Any other ideas on what's going on with whatever brought us over here? Or what brought me over here anyway," he corrected himself.

"I still feel that Leia's in danger, but I don't feel like it's necessarily connected to the ghost baby, it's possible the baby is part of it."

"Did you tell her that part of the reason the baby is in

danger is whatever this other issue is?"

"No," she admitted, "because then Bullard will lock her up in the bedroom and will keep her there, and it won't make a difference."

"No, and the trouble is, people who don't do this kind of energy work or have access to this kind of energy stuff just don't get it. When we feel things, that doesn't matter. We can do everything we can to try and stop it, but we can't always."

Lacy grimaced. "We just need to make sure that one of us is always with her."

"They are further improving the security today. Bullard's pretty pissed off at the holes that had opened up. *Getting lax* is how Bullard put it." Bojan had to smile. "So that's on top of the to-do list today."

"Yeah," she added, "and eventually I need to go back to my apartment. I didn't let it go because I wasn't sure how long I wanted to be here. I sublet it to a friend."

"What do you need?"

"I left a bunch of stuff in the guest bedroom, like my other clothes and some books I need."

"Will you really finish your education?"

"I *will* finish my education," she declared, with a nod. "If nothing else, it gives me validity in other people's eyes, which allows me access to people that are hurting."

He thought about that for a long moment. He didn't say anything but gave her a nod of understanding.

"I know it doesn't make sense to you," she shared, "but I still feel the need to do what I can."

"It's not that it doesn't make sense. It's just a matter of choosing those people we can help, since we can't help everyone," he reminded her. "If there were a way to teach more people to help others, then I would be all for it. However, working ourselves to the bone puts us at risk to potentially kill ourselves in the process. We need a better system." With that, he grabbed his towel and said, "I'll go get changed."

TO BOJAN, IT was more than about getting changed; it was about taking a break from being so close to Lacy. Having opened the mental door to their energy connection, it was like walking toward a ray of sunshine, knowing he should be comfortable with it because of the bond between them—yet finding it foreign after having closed that door on her for so long. It was so different, yet not different at all. It was brand-new and unique, to the point that he just wanted to pick her up, carry her to the field, and make love to her in the midst of the sunshine and flowers, until neither of them could move, but that wasn't an option. They were a hell of a long way from that.

Yet he knew it was their future, and that made life easier for him now, knowing that he wasn't alone and that he wasn't caught in the past. However, … at the same time, still something held him back. He wanted some excuse to say goodbye. Yet he didn't quite understand how he was supposed to do that. He just hoped there would be that option.

By the time he got changed and headed back downstairs, Dave called him over.

"I've got the ballistics back on that bullet. There is nothing in the databases, which isn't surprising. It was a .44," he added. Bojan nodded, as Dave frowned at him. "How are you holding up?"

"I'm holding," he said. "Sorry about yesterday. It's not that we wanted to share all that personal stuff, but we didn't know quite how to clear the air, and everybody deserved an explanation."

"Well, I don't know that anybody deserved an explanation, but it sure helped us all to understand what you guys were going through," Dave acknowledged. "As somebody who also lost an entire family …" Dave paused for a moment, then took a deep breath and continued. "Believe me. I do understand what you've been through, and learning to say goodbye and to move on is one of the hardest things anyone ever has to do."

"I still don't even know how to do that," Bojan shared, looking over at him. "I feel as if I haven't said my goodbyes, and that is still holding me back. I just don't quite know how to get past it. I mean, how do you say goodbye to a part of your heart?" he asked, holding back the emotions threatening to choke him. "I know that I can't bring her or the baby back, and believe me, I hated myself for not being able to do that. As energy workers, we have the ability to do so much. Yet, at the same time, we don't have the ability to cross that line. So there's always a feeling of being inadequate, of not being enough when it really counts, and that's very hard to live with."

"Of course it is," Dave agreed roughly. "I mean, you may just need to take a moment in silence and talk to her, tell her that it's time to let her go, but that you'll never forget her or replace her. I don't know whether she, in her physical form, would have understood or not, but I can tell you that I do believe *in spirit form* they totally understand." And with that, Dave added, "You'll have to work on that. However, in the meantime, breakfast seems like a good choice, though it's getting closer to lunch, I guess. So, are you up for brunch?"

"I'm here," he said, "although we normally eat a lot earlier."

"Yes, I think Leia and Lacy kind of changed that this morning."

"Right," Bojan mumbled, with a wry look. "Lacy does have a habit of switching things around."

"She brings life to everything," Dave noted, "and that is not a bad thing."

As they walked into the kitchen, Bojan noted another woman there.

Dave walked over, gave her a kiss, and she wrapped her arms around him. She teased him by saying, "I know you're just here because I took cinnamon buns out of the oven."

He gave her a second big kiss and muttered, "Maybe."

Then she laughed and said, "Get to the table. The food's on." She looked over at Bojan. "Hey, we haven't met yet." She introduced herself. "I'm Katie, Dave's partner," she murmured. "Whatever you had to say last night really hit him like a ton of bricks."

Bojan nodded. "Yes, and I'm sorry about that."

"Don't be. The more he accepts and understands and deals with things, the easier it is on him," she explained. "We can never take away your pain. All we can do is be there and make the days that you're not in pain as nice as they can be. Hopefully enough that you'll want to stay with us," she added.

Bojan sighed.

"Don't ever apologize for what you've been through," she told him. "Just pick up your feet and keep on walking. It's all any of us can do. And, on those notes of wisdom," she quipped, looking back to the ovens, "if you want cinnamon buns, you will have to get your ass out there because they will all be gone otherwise."

Bojan watched her carrying two massive trays. "Let me grab one of those."

She waited for him to take the top tray and teased, "That's just your way of making sure you get one, right? Don't think for a moment I haven't seen that move before."

"Absolutely," he admitted, with a wolfish grin. "You go first."

She rolled her eyes and walked out to the dining room, where everybody was filling their plates with bacon and eggs and sausage and ham. When she placed the cinnamon buns in the center of the table, everyone grabbed at least one. Before she had a chance to let people know about them, the first tray was gone. She put down the second tray, but two were already missing, which Bojan had snagged and put on his plate. She burst out laughing. "Well, I'm glad to see there's nothing slow about you, so you won't starve in this place."

"That situation is the same in every place with a crew like this." Then he quickly found a place to sit down. After everybody was settled in and the sounds of happy munchers filled the room, Bullard looked over at him.

"You got any idea what the danger is that we're supposed to be watching out for?" he asked, staring as he spoke. "It's pretty hard to look for an attacker if we have no idea what's even happening and why."

"I know." Bojan hesitated for a moment, then shared, "Lacy mentioned it earlier to Leia, but the gifts of the two of us are stronger if we're together."

"So, in that case, I suggest we go over the files and lists

of people and cases again, and see what we come up with."

"I already pointed out the pertinent one," Bojan stated, glancing back at Bullard.

Bullard nodded. "You did, but we didn't have any specifics to go on. No connections can be made until we do. I understand how the killing doc getting caught would bring Leia in his crosshairs, but he already had his eyes on her for years."

"Right. We need to know what else is related to that case. I can do some digging on that. Meanwhile, I understand you're doing the upgrade on the tech issues with the security system today?" he asked, looking over at Bullard.

Bullard nodded. "I just purchased the property next door last night," he declared, with a growl. "We will set up security on that one too."

Stunned, Bojan stared at Bullard, wondering at a man who would turn around and purchase acres of property because it bordered his place. But Bullard was all about security and didn't like the failure that had resulted in Lacy being shot. "That sounds good," Bojan replied. "You guys work on that, and Lacy and I will take a look at everybody involved in your world in the last little while." He looked over at Dave. "You have security camera footage available, right?"

"I do. How far back do you want to go?"

He hesitated, then he looked over at Lacy, who had just joined them. "I'll say two weeks. What do you think?"

Lacy nodded. "That's probably a good idea."

Leia frowned, looking at him. "It never occurred to me to look at the security cameras."

"That's because you're living here, used to seeing a certain amount of new faces," he muttered. "I've just arrived.

The security, the people, the faces, they won't be ones I know, so I won't have preconceived notions about them. I can go see what comes up from my energy reading on that."

Lacy nodded. "Okay, agreed, we can do that afterward."

And, with that, they went back to eating. After a moment, Ryland added, "And if you guys come up with anything that we can do—"

"Right. There is one other thing." Bojan hesitated for a moment, then looked down the table and up at Bullard. "I did get an odd feeling with the shooter. This sense of familiarity to him."

Bullard put down his fork and stared at him. "What do you mean?"

"This whole mess, I think, was meant as a warning shot, and I think the message was intended for whoever got it, so not necessarily Leia herself. But it *was* a warning, so I'm wondering if there isn't something in the background that you have thought wasn't a threat but is. I know that's fairly convoluted, and I'm not trying to be vague, but, because of the familiarity issue, I think it's probably somebody you know."

With that, Bullard reached for a cinnamon bun, his face twisted in fierce concentration, as he thought about it. "The trouble is, I know hundreds if not thousands of people, so I would need that narrowed down," he shared. "Plus, how does this tie in with the doc killing from so many years ago?"

"Six degrees of separation," Ryland muttered.

"Right," Bojan concurred. "You go back far enough, and you might find the connection. I will start by taking a look at the recent camera feed to see if anybody could be of concern. Then we can work backward and see what we find."

Bullard frowned. "Among the thousands that I know?

Good luck with that."

Bojan refilled his coffee cup, snagged his plate with the cinnamon buns, then looked over at Lacy.

She stood up and nodded. "I'm ready."

And without the need to converse verbally, the two of them walked out.

CHAPTER 8

LACY HEARD THE dining room chatter increase as she and Bojan left. She looked over at him and asked, "I wonder how much the conversation behind us will change."

He shrugged. "We can expect them to talk."

"I know they're curious and confused, just like the rest of us," she muttered.

"Absolutely," he agreed, with a knowing smile, "but we are a step closer to where we're supposed to be, so that's a good thing."

She held his comment close, wondering if he really was at the point where he could acknowledge where they were at and could go forward from here. She didn't want to push it, as she still felt a little raw and on the bruised side.

As they walked over to the security room, Dave met them there and let them in, setting them up in front of a pair of monitors. "I'll replay the last two weeks," he began, "and you can control the speed, as you like." And, with that, he turned and walked out, leaving them alone.

Lacy settled back to study the monitors and the faces as they flashed back and forth. Just because she'd been here over those two weeks, that didn't mean she necessarily knew everybody who had come and gone.

There were workers; there were delivery people; there were friends; there were the clinic patients. A lot of people lived here on a regular basis, but still Lacy hadn't come in contact with all of Bullard's crew. Working in the clinic kept her busy most days. Plus everybody else had a life here, and Lacy was a guest in that odd position of belonging but not quite belonging. She was doing a practicum here, which made her more of an employee than anything else. Yet, at the same time, it didn't feel anything like that kind of relationship.

She and Bojan quickly went through the video, but, on day four, he leaned forward, hit the Stop button, backed it up, and took a look at a man who was coming forward, dropping off a parcel, and talking to whoever received it, with a seemingly cheerful note. Then he walked away, everything completely normal. However, as he got to his vehicle, he stopped and turned back around and gave the one-finger salute to the house.

"Interesting," Lacy murmured. "Is that just somebody pissed off at someone having all this or is it more than that?"

"What do you think?" he asked, glancing over at her.

"I vote for more than that," she said instantly. "I'm just not exactly sure what we're looking at here."

Bojan went forward on the tape again, and they watched to see if anything else came on strong enough to point them anywhere else. Bojan noted, "That delivery driver didn't come back either, in the next ten days."

She frowned, as Bojan rewound the tape to the spot where the delivery driver was, and they went through the tape again. "Do you think Bullard knows him?" Lacy asked.

"It's possible," Bojan replied. "I'll run that face through facial recognition and see if we get anything."

"It still blows me away that facial recognition is even something we have access to here," she murmured.

"Nothing is common about Bullard and his team, or the other teams he's connected to, and I think that, for the most part, many governments are happy to keep them in technology, as they keep them safe as well."

"I wouldn't be at all surprised," she murmured, leaning forward, studying the delivery guy. "It's a regular delivery vehicle. It's got plates. I'm sure it will check out. We know he was here. He was probably doing rounds or at least filled in for somebody for the day or just even for that moment," she suggested. "So the question is, was that finger salute something he expected people to see and to recognize as being a threat, or was something else going on?"

"*Hmm.* I would say something else is going on," Bojan declared, as he showed her the screen on his laptop and the facial recognition program that came up almost immediately. "He's wanted by Interpol."

Startled, she turned and glanced at him. "Seriously?"

He tapped the monitor again, redirecting her gaze to the mug shot on the screen.

She looked from one image to the other and then slowly nodded. "Okay, so this guy is obviously somebody we need to sort out, but who is he? And what's his problem here? Why is it that nobody here sensed there was an issue?"

"Because nobody saw him, nobody recognized him as anything more than a delivery guy. It's not as if you can run facial recognition software from your front door," he muttered.

"Yet obviously they should be," she muttered right back at him.

He laughed. "Wouldn't that be nice, however, but impractical. It would be way too cumbersome and, in most cases, never an issue. Obviously, in this case, something is going on here that Bullard needs to see." At that, he got up with his laptop in his hands and headed out the door to where everybody was gathered.

She followed behind, wondering at the lack of psychic communication. Then she heard a pounding in her mind. She headed toward the next door to the adjoining room.

Bojan sighed and said out loud, "Maybe let's try that again."

She looked over at him. "What?"

"Open the damn door."

She looked at the physical door nearby, turning to frown at him, and then thought about the mental door between them, finally popping it open.

Much better, he murmured in her head. *Now at least we're on the same wavelength.*

"Have you been trying to talk to me telepathically the whole time?" she asked with amusement, as she headed behind him to the kitchen.

"Yes, and you haven't been answering. I figured it was stubbornness, but now I realize the door was closed."

"Well, just because you opened the door on your side," she stated, "doesn't mean I opened the door on mine."

He stopped and stared at her. Then, with a nod, he replied, "Good point, so, if you want to shut it again, you'll let me know, *huh*?"

At that, she turned, realizing several people still stood around, looking at the two of them talking among themselves, wondering what was going on.

She smiled at them and shook her head. "Don't worry, just a communication glitch."

"Yeah, like telepathic or what?" Ryland asked in fascination. "Can you guys do that?"

"Yes, as long as she opens the damn door in her mind," Bojan muttered.

At that, she laughed. "And maybe that's something that *she* has to get around to doing."

"Yeah, and, as long as *she* does it fast, we'll be fine," he muttered.

She snorted. "The door is open, but I'll feel free to close it when I want to."

"Good," Bojan declared. "Ditto on both sides."

Fascinated, everybody was looking from one to the other, until Bullard walked in, staring at the laptop in front of them, and asked, "What's going on?"

Bojan pointed, then asked, "Do you know this man?"

Bullard looked at the mug shot photo and nodded. "Yeah, I sure do. I worked with him in the military many, many years ago. At one point in time, I even tried hiring him, but ended up firing him."

"Yeah, and why didn't it work out?" Bojan asked.

"I don't remember," Bullard said, looking at him. "It just didn't work out."

"Well, you will need to give it some thought and jog your memory a little," Bojan declared, switching screens, "because this guy was at your front door, delivering a parcel eight days ago."

Bullard's gaze widened in shock, and he said, "What?" He quickly came closer to look down at the screen, as Bojan played the clip and showed him the delivery as well as the one-finger salute.

"Holy crap." Bullard stared at it. He pulled the laptop closer, then went back and forth between the two images several times. "That's definitely Charlie, but I don't know why he's pissed off at me. What the hell did he deliver?"

"That is the next question we have to find the answer to. Who would have received the delivery? Who would have brought in something from somebody like that? Does anybody check out your parcels or do any screening?"

Bullard frowned at him. "No, and no," he muttered. "Thanks for reminding me once again how lax everything's gotten."

"It's only lax until there's a problem, and right now you have a problem."

"Do we? Are you sure?"

"Yes, we're really sure, and it's related to this guy. We just don't know what his endgame is. If we knew what he delivered, it might help. We also need to find out whether this guy works for a delivery company or took over the job for the day, and, if so, where is the regular driver? We'd want to have a conversation with him too."

"Well, shit," Bullard muttered.

Ryland hopped up and offered, "You don't have to handle that. You need to look after surgeries today in the clinic and stay close to Leia. So Dave and I will jump in on this with Bojan."

When Bullard looked over at him, Bojan nodded. "Absolutely," Bojan replied. "We need to track down this guy and have a talk with him as soon as possible."

Ryland agreed. "I'm on it." And, with that, he walked out of the room.

Bojan added, "And you need to jog your brain for what was going on with this guy all those years ago."

Bullard looked over at Bojan. "Shit."

"Listen. It doesn't matter who does what at this point," Bojan noted. "We just need to get down to the basics, put protocols in place, and get set up in case something more is happening that we don't know about. We've got to implement some sort of security plan for anybody coming on or around the property."

"We've got a start on that," Bullard stated. "We've closed the doors and gates, and nobody is allowed in until they pass the security clearance. That used to be our standard procedure, but, after I came back from the island and that whole thing was resolved, we relaxed the level of security. We have so many people living here and others coming to access the clinic that it was easier. … Obviously right now it's not so fine."

"No, not so fine, and all that definitely needs to be reinstated," Bojan muttered.

Nodding, Bullard looked a bit frazzled.

"No worries," Dave said. "I'll ensure that's made clear to everyone and that we get the infrastructure in place today."

At that, Dave and Bojan both disappeared, leaving Lacy standing here in the middle of the room. She turned to Bullard. "How's Leia?"

"Leia's fine," he said. "I just spoke to her, and she's had a nap. She's coming down to get a bit more food. Are you okay to help in the clinic today?"

Lacy nodded. "Sure, I can do that."

"Good," Bullard replied. "That's where I'm heading now."

And, with that, she turned and followed him into the clinic, checking the schedule—everything from a minor thing, like removing stitches, to somebody who had called in first thing this morning after splitting their knee in a bike accident, plus a mixed bag of other procedures. She sighed and quickly started prepping the room.

"Are you okay?" Bullard asked, from behind her.

"I'm fine," she replied. "It's just one of those *heavy thoughts* days, you know?"

"Yeah, I do know, and believe me. I'm not at all sure I should even be in here."

"No, you definitely should be," she countered. "This is the best way to put Leia at ease about not being here herself. Let your team have a chance to do what they do best, and we'll keep things going here."

He nodded but didn't say anything more about it.

It was an uneasy two hours later before she turned around and checked the schedule, realizing they were finished for a while.

"You've done great today," Bullard noted.

"I don't know," she murmured, starting to straighten things up. "I was afraid I would be too distracted, after all that's happened."

"If anything, you seem to be more, … I don't know, smoother, really stable. More focused even."

She laughed. "It sounds as if you're trying to say I was a mess before?"

Chuckling, he shook his head. "No, I was not trying to say anything along those lines, but you do seem to be calmer and more settled in a way that you weren't before."

"Well, it's likely that I'll be more settled each day, as I get more distance from all that's happened. It'll just take some time to adjust. Probably by next week, things will be working just fine."

"Well, if today is an example, you are working just fine right now. So, if you will improve even more, that's awesome. I was considering having you stay on full-time, but, according to Leia, you feel the need to go to Terk's place in England."

"I do," she confirmed, "or at least split my time somehow. I strongly feel the need to go help them out." Then she stopped and looked off into the distance, frowning.

"What?"

"Something about a pediatrician, but I'm not sure what that means either." She shrugged. "A pediatrician is coming into play over there at Terk's compound as well, but I don't know any more than that."

"Sounds like they need one," Bullard quipped, with a big grin.

"Yeah, they sure do, and, of course, unlike you, Terkel's not a surgeon."

"I'm a roughneck surgeon," Bullard clarified. "And legally there are definitely some things that hold me back. But Leia and her expertise has all that taken care of." Bullard gave a wave of his hands. "So it's all good."

Lacy laughed. "It's not as if you will let anybody stop you from doing something anyway."

"When it comes down to all those surgical niceties, I'm glad to be here at my own clinic because those issues aren't so much a problem, and just being able and willing to help sick and injured people are enough credentials. Yet I didn't want to risk Leia giving birth just anywhere, just in case."

"Right," Lacy agreed, "but you really love it here?"

"I do, though managing multiple holdings is more complicated, particularly now that I have a growing family. So I need to decide whether I will set up more holdings or just consolidate and stick to this main one."

"You have a big team though, so maybe you should be asking some of them if they want to move."

"It's under discussion and has been for a while," he admitted. "When you think about it, having everybody here can be a little bit cramped too, now that so many of the team have partners. There is always talk of setting up in Australia as well," he noted, with a smile, "but Tabi, Ryland's partner, is heading that one."

"Is that where she is from?"

"It is. In fact, she's over there right now," Bullard stated. "I think we'll just have a team that keeps shifting around, sometimes here, sometimes over there, maybe even settling here for five years, ten years, and then shifting over there too," he suggested, with a shrug. "Nothing wrong with that, as lots of good places to live are all over this world. And, with the communication modes we have these days, it's even easier to stay in touch."

"Yeah, you're not kidding," she muttered. At that, Terkel knocked on the door in her brain. She frowned, stopping in the middle of the room. *Terkel? You don't generally knock.*

Yeah, but you put up some barriers, and I didn't know whether it was against me or Bojan, Terk explained, with a note of humor. *So, I was attempting to follow the protocols that you were attempting to put into place.*

She laughed, Bullard eyeing her now. *Yeah, it's not as if anybody will ever listen to any protocols I put into place. You guys just ignore me.*

Maybe we're just trying to take some of that into account, Terk suggested. *And pay attention to a mother dying of cancer. Anyway, I'm really checking in to see how Leia is doing.*

Something was off in his voice, so she turned and looked at Bullard. "When did you see Leia last?" she asked Bullard.

"A couple hours ago. Why?" As he put down the last of the surgical instruments on the tables, gleaming and ready, he asked, "Is there a problem?"

"No, Terkel's checking in on her."

"Well, Terkel can check in on her without going through us," Bullard noted shrewdly, "so what's the problem?" At that, he stiffened and walked out. "Leia! Leia?"

Lacy rushed to follow Bullard and added, "I'm not saying anything is wrong, but, because of the issue with Bojan, I shut some doors in my head." Bullard looked at her, with a strange expression. She shrugged. "Terk's just checking in to make sure Leia's doing okay."

At that, Leia came out of the kitchen, a phone to her ear. She quickly ended the call and asked, "What's the matter?"

"Are you okay?" Bullard asked her.

"I'm fine," she said, with a reassuring smile. "But trying to get a second crib? That's a whole different story."

"We could wait," he reminded her.

"No, we won't wait," she declared. "If he needs to know that he's welcome and wanted, we will have a welcome wagon in place." She looked over at Lacy. "Sorry about that. Just one more insight into family life that you can't get away from when you live here."

"Understood." Lacy looked over at Bullard. "Listen. I'll finish cleaning up the clinic and will leave you guys alone." With that, she quickly escaped once again, worrying that she shouldn't have brought it up in the first place. But, at least with the proper information, people could make better decisions for themselves. It was so hard when there was nothing she could do. It was partly why she had felt so helpless all this time with Bojan. Although she had the information and knew what he was going through, she couldn't help him, and it had made for a pretty rough go-round.

But she was still better off knowing that's what he'd been going through, while biding his time. Now that things had technically changed, everything else had changed as well. She just didn't know to what extent.

She walked into the kitchen and put on a pot of tea, then turned to see Pia standing there, talking on the phone. It seemed that everybody was on the phone today. She smiled when he got off, and he turned in surprise to see her. "Sorry, I didn't mean to interrupt your phone call."

He shook his head. "I was just calling my brother. Your shared story reminded me that time is too short and that we don't always get a chance to talk to our loved ones as much as we might want to."

She looked at him in surprise, then nodded. "If it helps bring people together, then I guess I'm okay that our story ended up being a little more public than I would have liked."

He laughed. "Nothing's ever easy about having details of our personal lives brought out into the open. However, in this case, some good has definitely come out of it. I know of several who have reached out to try and open some lines of communication that were previously closed, so it's all good."

She smiled. "Thank you for that. I just put the kettle on for tea," she murmured. "I'll go finish up in the surgery suite and get ready for the afternoon."

"Do you need food?" he asked.

She shook her head. "No, I ate a lot at breakfast, so I'm good, at least for another hour or two." When he frowned at her, she laughed. "It's not the medical work that burns up my energy. It's the energy work."

"Are you doing much of that?"

"I can't do a whole lot without freaking people out and getting accused of doing all kinds of voodoo witchcraft things," she shared. "So, in the clinic, we're pretty much just stitching people up and helping them out as best we can. It's one thing to add a touch of magic to the healing process, but I can't go too far."

"Right." Pia nodded, as he stared out the window. "I guess it really does confuse things."

"It absolutely does, but that's okay because confusing things isn't necessarily bad. It's just a matter of keeping it up and making the right decisions." She looked around and asked, "Nobody back yet?"

"No, nobody is back yet." He studied her carefully. "But you knew that, right?"

"Yes, I do know that, but again it becomes part of the conversation, doesn't it?"

He smiled. "And keeps a part of the conversation out loud. Otherwise, when you start going off, talking in your own private world, it gets a little freaky for everybody else."

"You're right," she agreed, "and that's a little hard on us because it's instinctive to talk that way now. Once I opened the door …"

"You were right to keep it closed, although he seems to be a changed man at the moment."

"I think he's had an epiphany of sorts, if I can put it that way," she replied. "Now that he's on that pathway, it's up to me to open the doors myself—doors that I hadn't realized I had kept so tightly closed."

Pia nodded at her, understanding. "Self-preservation is something all of us instinctively do."

"Isn't that the truth? Anyway, I'm heading back to work now."

And, with her fresh pot of tea, she returned to the clinic area, not surprised to find it empty. She quickly finished setting up for the afternoon, and, when she still saw no sign of Bullard, she went looking for him. She found him in the kitchen, snapping into the phone. She waited until he was off, and he turned and glared at her.

When he saw it was her, he sighed. "Don't tell me that I need to come help you."

"Unless you're planning on me doing all the surgical procedures today," she noted, stopping to roll her eyes, "otherwise, yeah, you need to come."

He nodded. "Lead the way." Again he sighed, and that started the rest of her afternoon.

TRACKING DOWN THE shooter had proven to be way too easy, and, by the time Bojan, Ryland, and Dave had pulled up at his apartment, Bojan got out and looked at the building, then shook his head. "Something about this feels wrong."

The others stopped and frowned at him. "Well, in that case, you tell us what we're doing," Ryland said, crossing his arms atop the car hood. "Because, if you say something is wrong here, believe me. None of us are going into that building until you say something is right."

Dave nodded.

Bojan looked at them, then shrugged. "I don't sense danger, but I also don't sense a solution to our problem."

Dave nodded. "Good enough, let's go figure out why." And, with that, the trio walked up to the apartment and knocked on the door but got no answer.

Ryland lifted his chin. "That fits with what you told us."

"Yes and no." Bojan stared at the door.

"What's the matter, man?" Dave asked.

"Somebody's in there all right," Bojan shared, his tone

thick with emotions, "but I'm not getting any sense of life."

At that, Ryland quickly pulled a little tool set from his back pocket and popped open the door. The smell hit them immediately. "Well shit," he muttered.

Bojan nodded. "Yeah, I should have seen that from outside. I didn't open it up that much." He shook his head.

"What?" Dave asked.

"I have to admit that things are a little bit off just because of the changes."

"Off how? Stronger, weaker, or what?" Ryland asked.

"Stronger, but the messages are a little bit more confused. So I guess *off* in the sense that clarity could be a little lacking."

"*Great*," Ryland muttered.

"On the other hand," Bojan added cheerfully, "we're definitely way stronger this way. So, even if it's a little inconvenient, it's not bad." They wandered through the apartment to find the occupant in bed with a bullet in his head. He had obviously been there a day or two, based on the decay.

"Is this even the guy we're looking for?" Ryland asked.

Bojan shook his head. "Nope, it's not." He wandered to the other bedroom and pointed out, "This is where the shooter was staying." They stepped up to see a completely empty bedroom, with the bedding still tossed, half on the floor and half hanging off the bed.

"So, what then? He shot his roommate and walked?" Dave asked.

"That's what it looks like," Bojan replied, "but why?"

"Because he expected to be tracked, that's why," Ryland stated.

"But maybe not," Bojan argued. "If Lacy hadn't been

shot, we wouldn't have any idea that our shooter was even around. So maybe the warning shot was less of a warning and more of a nudge to get our heads in the game and to acknowledge the shooter exists." At that, Ryland and Dave looked at Bojan and frowned. He shrugged. "Just think about it. If he sent something—like that delivery he made to the compound—and no one saw or opened it, he'd be pissed off that after nine or ten days, no one at the compound had picked up whatever gauntlet he thought he'd thrown down. Thus, shooting Lacy was more like his way of dragging us into the ring. He wanted to make a statement, such as, *I'm serious. Stop treating me as if I don't matter*, you know?"

"Now that rings true," Ryland agreed. "I can see some of the guys we've dealt with in the past feeling that way. Do you know this guy?" Ryland asked Bojan.

"No, I don't know anything about him," Bojan replied. "Bullard knows a bit. Hopefully he'll remember more."

Dave spoke up. "We pulled this guy's history and found Charlie's got an erratic record, working as a mercenary for various groups, but a few years back that stopped as well."

"Maybe he got injured," Bojan suggested. "Injured or deemed too unstable for employment."

"Either way that makes sense," Dave noted. "So now we're looking at someone who's potentially blaming Bullard for something, and, while we don't know what for, it could just be the shooter's circumstances in life that he's pissed off about. Maybe he thinks Bullard is to blame for it somehow."

Bojan nodded. "Bullard said he hired Charlie but had to fire him. So something was back there even a decade or so ago."

Dave added, "Agreed. Or it could be completely unrelated and have something to do with Bullard's own history. Or it could be nothing that makes sense at all," he added.

"Exactly, so we're not getting very far," Ryland pointed out.

"No, we're not getting very far," Dave agreed, "but, by the same token, Charlie's mostly likely good for the murder of his roommate, whoever he was."

Ryland added, "The other option is that Charlie skipped town before somebody else he'd pissed off came looking for him."

"Oh, I like that theory," Bojan stated. "It has a ring of truth to it."

"A ring of truth?" Dave questioned.

Bojan nodded. "If Charlie was looking to start something, would he have done it with just Bullard, or would he have done it with multiple people, maybe other past employers or contacts who fired him or let him go? Remember how his bio was filled with a lot of job hopping? Maybe Charlie was looking for money, for a payout from Bullard. ... What we need to know is more about that parcel he dropped off and any repercussions from that."

"Meaning?" Dave asked.

"Meaning that," Bojan explained, "if our shooter dropped something off, and it was meant to be a threat, but it was ignored, then Charlie would most likely be pissed off because he wanted validation and some kind of reaction. But, if he did it to more than one person—such as all his former employers—but we were a little slower to pick up the ball, maybe that other person tried to take out Charlie but got his roommate instead. And, with some warning that our shooter was about to get in trouble, maybe he skipped out, maybe without warning his roommate, or maybe came back and found the roommate dead, and now our shooter is all in."

"Any of that is possible," Dave agreed, "but we should report this to the police, before we do anything else."

"You have somebody for that, don't you?" Bojan asked.

"We do," Ryland muttered, "a local LEO, not that he's ever that happy to see us."

"Sounds like Jonas over in MI6," Bojan pointed out. "He's basically Terkel's handler, even if it involves MI5, not just his own department."

At that, Dave laughed. "I think Jonas has become the handler for all of us in some ways. He takes the hit if we screw up, so he's always on our case, making sure we don't do anything that comes back on him. So, yeah, he's always involved it seems, no matter what it is that we're up to or whatever country we're in."

"So now that Terkel's gone private, he's doing jobs for Jonas," Bojan shared, with a big smile. "As I understand it, the British government is becoming a steady source of income for them."

At that, Ryland shook his head. "Whoever would have thought that would happen? But it makes sense that Terk's team went private, after they got screwed over so badly by their government."

"Yeah, you're not kidding," Bojan muttered, "in every possible way." At that, the others just nodded. Stepping out of the bedroom into the hallway, Bojan stated, "We need to see if anybody saw where this guy went. We can pull from street cams outside to see what vehicle he was driving, and then we need to find out if anybody has a clue who this dead guy is and what may have been his relationship with our shooter."

"I'm getting the team on all that right now," Ryland

said, as he started punching numbers into his phone, starting with Riff's, and received an almost instant response. *Outside on guard. You'll see me when you see me.*

"Good enough," Bojan replied. "Now we have to figure out what's next." As he turned, one of the doors opened down the hallway, and somebody stepped out, saw them there, and quickly raced back inside. "Looks like we're starting right here."

CHAPTER 9

B Y THE END of the day, Lacy had checked in several times with Bojan's energy, but everything had been fine. Frustrated, she quickly hopped back out of his mind, so as not to intrude. Setting boundaries was a huge part of any relationship, but, with something like theirs, it was an even bigger issue, and she knew they were already in danger of crossing those kinds of boundaries on a regular basis, when they weren't comfortable with this relationship just yet. Besides, they didn't even necessarily have a relationship, which she constantly pointed out to herself. Frankly that was getting a bit on the old side.

By the time she was done with her work in the clinic, she quickly changed into her swimming suit and headed out to the pool. She glanced around, knowing Bullard's extra security men were out there. She didn't see them, which was how it was meant to be. When she checked energywise, she noted the extra sources, but all checked out to be nonthreatening.

Leia was lounging in the shallow end. She looked up, smiled, and asked, "How did things go at the clinic today?"

"It wasn't bad at all. Traffic was steady with nothing major, nothing traumatizing," she replied, right before she dove into the pool. She broke through the cold, refreshing water on the other side and started doing laps. After she'd done twenty, she pulled up beside Leia and asked, "So, how are you doing?"

"I'm good," she said. "I'm thinking I should just wear a sign that says as much."

"People will continue to ask you anyway," Lacy noted, with a laugh, "so it would probably be a waste of energy, not to mention the waste of a perfectly good sign."

"Right, just because you're pregnant, everybody thinks you are ready to blow up."

"I think *blow out* might be a better phrase," Lacy muttered. "Everybody is just afraid you will have the babies while they're around, and honestly they all want to be far away."

At that, Leia burst out laughing. "That's probably true, isn't it?"

Lacy gave her a big, fat grin. "Hey, babies are not for everybody. Toddlers are good—and kids when they're fun and cute—but delicate newborns tend to make a lot of grown men pretty edgy."

"Well, they better all get used to it because I don't know of a single woman here who doesn't hope to have a family of her own, and an awful lot of people live here now."

"I understand that some of them will be moving?"

"Yeah, there will be changes," she acknowledged. "I think some of them will go to Australia. Some of them are moving over here. Some of them may switch out to our Tunisia base." She shrugged. "The Australia base is not even set up yet, in any formal fashion, but discussions are underway."

"So, you didn't want to go to Tunisia?"

She sighed. "It's his favorite location, but not mine," she admitted. "Though I would be totally okay with spending some time in Australia too."

"You like the climate?"

"I like this climate as well. I don't know what we'll end up doing, but I would like to be away from as much of this craziness as possible, particularly if we are raising a family."

"Nobody will slight you for that," Lacy noted. "So, you better tell him, and you might be surprised at his reaction too."

"Of course I always feel the pull to get back to my island," she shared, with a laugh, "but not until after the babies come."

"And probably not for a while after that either," Lacy stated, with a warning tone. "You will have your hands full."

"And that's another thing. I was wondering about hiring some people, but so many wonderful women are here already. Yet I didn't know if I should ask if any of them wanted to be involved in a bigger way."

"How would you feel about it if they were?" Lacy asked curiously.

"I would be totally fine with it. We have a really great relationship with everybody here," she shared. "We're so blessed honestly. We have been blessed in so many areas of life that sometimes I have to pinch myself, and part of me is afraid it'll all blow up in my face because it's not real."

"Understandable," Lacy agreed. "I find myself in that same situation right now."

At that, Leia looked at her in growing understanding. "You guys need some time together to sort it out, don't you?"

"We're getting there," she murmured. "At the same time, you're right. Time alone would be great, but it won't happen anytime soon."

She nodded. "You mentioned I would deliver *early*."

She waited and then nodded. "Yeah, *earlier*."

"But how much earlier?"

"Sorry, I don't have anything at the moment," Lacy said.

"Every day is a blessing," Leia repeated, as she settled back. "You would tell me if I needed to know something, right?"

"I already have," she declared, looking over at her. "And believe me. At times I worry that I did the wrong thing."

Leia shook her head. "No. You definitely did the right thing. How can we make a proper decision unless we are fully informed? We all have to make our own choices on how we will handle information like that, but we're still better to have it."

"Are we though? No doubt many people wouldn't agree."

"Well, as for me, I am grateful to know," Leia declared. "I'm working my way around to being accepting, if it doesn't go our way, and I have to admit to being quite thrilled to hear Bojan suggest the potential for another pregnancy in the future," she muttered. "I didn't think I would ever have this opportunity, and now I'm doubly blessed."

At that, Lacy looked at her friend and smiled. "You are blessed. Just keep remembering that, and let's hope that everything works out okay."

Leia sighed. "And, of course, knowing that you have some answers, that means I want *all* the answers."

Lacy burst out laughing. "If it were that easy, I would give them to you. But it isn't that easy, and I can't." Just then, the door opened, and Bullard walked out.

"There was a delivery," he began, looking at Leia, "ten or so days ago." He held out the delivery log and looked at her. "Do you remember what this guy dropped off?"

She looked at the log and frowned. "Good God, I have no idea."

"I also don't have any record of an order being placed and shipped by this delivery company," he added.

She winced. "Okay, that doesn't sound good."

"No, we had a lot of deliveries coming in that week in particular, but we also had an awful lot of family and other people delivering things too. I've checked with everybody who was here, and nobody has any record of this particular delivery."

"So, something was delivered by the shooter, I presume," Lacy noted, "but you don't know what it was, and that's likely why this guy is pissed off?"

Bullard stared at her, frowning. "Go on."

"If he thought that whatever he delivered would get a reaction or some sort of response, … and who knows, maybe any reaction would do," she explained. "However, if it didn't happen, so then shooting me was another message, like, *Hey, smarten up*, or something of that nature."

"Or maybe *Pay attention to me*," Leia suggested.

"Exactly," Lacy agreed. "I've been shot now, and we still didn't know what was going on. In retrospect, it's quite possible that he expected you to understand what it all meant from the beginning."

"Yet I don't," Bullard admitted, frowning at her. "I don't have a clue, other than recognizing Charlie as the shooter."

She nodded at that.

"By the way"—he looked over at Leia—"the guys went to the shooter's place and found his roommate dead, and there's no sign of our shooter."

"Roommate shot in the head," Lacy noted.

Bullard glanced at her sideways and nodded. "Did you just figure that out or—"

"I took a peek into Bojan's mind," she said.

"*Okay*," Bullard replied. "Is there anything in Bojan's mind that will help?"

She chuckled. "Not at the moment, though he's running through the possibilities." She pondered that. "I'm not sure."

"Well, … if there is anything, let me know. I mean, tracking this guy *stat* would be the best idea. We better find out what the hell he wants, but, with his roommate dead, it could mean our shooter killed him, or somebody else killed him, or suicide."

"They don't think it was a suicide," Lacy stated, frowning, staring off in the distance.

"Which means," Bullard added, "either Charlie, our delivery guy and shooter, did it himself, or somebody else did it. So, the question is, why would Charlie shoot his own roommate? Maybe if the roommate was a partner in crime, and things blew up, or maybe the roommate wanted to turn in Charlie for his own crimes. Who knows? Maybe Charlie just got pissed off. I mean, I had to fire him like ten years ago because he had some real anger issues back then. I haven't had much interaction with him since then. So I don't know what our shooter's mental stability level is like in today's terms."

At that, Lacy paused, frowning. "I think I do know what his mental state is like, and it's not … sane," she shared, slowly standing up. "Let me talk to Bojan real quick." Then she closed her eyes, reached out to Bojan, and, with the finesse of a bull in a china shop, she slammed into his mind and asked, *The energy you picked up from the doorway after I was shot, did that have the energy of a sane mind?*

Bojan responded, *It was splintered, like fractured somehow, but I don't know what that means. I'm not used to picking up that kind of energy.*

She winced. *I'm wondering whether we might have somebody with brain damage or maybe on medication or something along that line. Maybe he sees Bullard as some kind of a bad guy. Or maybe Leia.*

Lacy came back to full awareness to find Bullard and Leia both staring at her, their curiosity evident in their expressions. Lacy hesitated a moment. "Is it possible Charlie sees Leia as a replacement or as the wrong partner for you somehow?"

Bullard stared at her. "What? No, I don't think so. … It's not as if I've had any serious relationships over the years, largely because of the work I do," he said, by way of explanation.

"I get that, but something's off about this shooter guy, and I'm just wondering whether he believes that you let him or somebody in his family down in some way."

"Well, I had to fire Charlie because he wasn't doing the work he needed to do, and he was definitely unstable at the time," Bullard noted, tilting his head to study her curiously. "There was something wrong with him, and I couldn't quite figure out what, but that was many years ago. It was pretty heated when I let him go, and he took off. I've not really heard any more about him … until now."

She nodded. "It makes you wonder *why now*, if all this happened in the past."

"Exactly."

"Unless somebody helped to keep him balanced and sane," Leia suggested, "and now something has happened to his caregiver maybe, interrupting that somehow."

Bullard hesitated. "He had a sister he was pretty close to, at one time."

"That would make sense. Do you want to see if you can track down the sister?"

"Yeah, I'm on it," he said, eyeing the logs of all the recent deliveries in his hand. "I'm still stumped about what Charlie would have delivered, as in something personal from him to me. Nothing among these noted deliveries jumps out on that. You guys toss that around, while I go see if I can rustle up a contact number for the sister." And, with that, he took off, leaving the two women on their own.

Lacy looked at Leia thoughtfully. "What's the protocol on the parcel delivery here?"

"In general all parcels must be signed for and are just left in the front hall. Anybody who is expecting something generally picks it up, or, if the deliveries begin to stack up, somebody will let people know that parcels are here for them. There should have been a name on that delivery, and, if it was for Bullard, somebody should have let him know it was there."

At that, Lacy nodded. "I'll go check the front hallway."

"Surely you don't think it's still there?" Leia asked curiously. "That would have been several days ago now."

"Depending on how big it is, it may have gotten overlooked or misplaced somehow." Lacy shrugged. "It won't hurt to go check."

With that, she walked inside and headed toward the front door. She passed several people working in the living room, trying to track down information. When she got to the entry area, she stopped near the big double doors, and even now a stack of parcels sat there for various team members. As she went through them, nothing had Bullard's name on it. Just to be sure, she looked behind and under the furniture in the area. Under the bench that sat in the entryway, she found a small envelope with Bullard's name on it.

She picked it up, knowing instinctively it was from that same energy. She walked over to where Bullard sat with several of his team and held it out. "I think this is what he delivered."

He frowned at her, then at the envelope, as it if were some snake ready to strike. "Where did you find that?"

"It was still in the front hall but had fallen under the bench."

He stared at her and then took it from her. "I presume there are already fingerprints all over it," he noted, staring at it carefully.

"I would assume so. I didn't necessarily sense any danger, but it is from him. I got the same energy as from when the moron shot me. At the moment, I'm not getting anything off this."

"It's not even sealed. There is no return address, no stamps, no nothing?"

"Nope. But it's addressed to you," she noted, with a big fat smile, "so the next move is yours."

He snorted at that. "Yeah? Well, I would take a holiday with my wife if I could."

"And you will have to soon enough because there will be babies."

At that, he bolted to his feet and asked, "Is she in labor?"

"No." Lacy groaned. "Sit down already."

"Good God." He collapsed back into his chair, glaring at her.

"Stop taking everything so literally. And, for the record,

she won't pop today."

"Yeah, you say that now, but then you say she will be early," he muttered, with a frown. "What do you expect us all to do?"

She laughed. "I expect you to calm down and to let the babies come in their own time."

"Well, that'll be fine," he groused, "so stop telling us it will be early."

"Right," she said, with an eye roll. "I'll stop telling you anything."

"Hey, that's not fair," he protested, turning the envelope in his hands before dumping the contents onto the table. There on top was a picture of a beautiful woman. He picked it up, staring at it, then looked at the back of the photo, where there was a notation. *"She's still waiting."*

"What the hell does that mean?" Lacy asked.

"I'm not sure," Bullard said, "but that's Charlie's sister."

"That brings us back to the same question that came up earlier. Did you have a relationship with her?" Leia asked, as she walked into the room, studying the photo.

"I did, yes," he admitted, with a sigh, "but we're talking about something that was an awfully long time ago, like fifteen or more years back."

"Yet some people don't ever really forget," Leia murmured. "If this woman was the person who kept Charlie stable and something happened to change that, maybe that has set him off somehow. Particularly if he is thinking you were supposed to look after her, to protect her somehow, or, I don't know, be with her maybe," she added. "That could certainly explain the threat against me." When she looked to Lacy for validation, Lacy nodded.

Bullard looked over at his team. Each nodded.

"Charlie's decline is definitely connected to that woman, and you were looking for a way to contact her, right?" Lacy asked.

"Yes, but there's a date on this, so, if she's deceased, it's only just recently happened. Sit tight and let me check on this." Stepping away, Bullard made a series of phone calls. He came back and nodded. "She was killed several days ago," he told everyone, "like fourteen days ago."

"About ten days ago Charlie would have probably just buried her," Leia suggested, "and would be sitting there alone, wondering at the emotions in his life, particularly if he's on medications and his sister was looking after him."

"Yeah, I've got a phone call in to his doctor right now," Bullard said. "We should have answers very soon." Pacing for a moment, he looked over at the women again. "The problem is, we didn't even see this letter, but honestly I don't know that, even if I had, I would have understood what it was all about."

Lacy spoke up. "No, but you might have looked into it or at least recognized the photo and realized that somebody you had known had passed away. Maybe he was expecting you to reach out. Maybe he was expecting …" She stopped and shrugged. "I don't know, but, if he has a broken mind, he would be even less likely to cope with his loss and to understand what was happening, much less to reach out in a more rational way."

Bullard nodded. When the phone rang, he hopped up. "It's his doctor." He quickly identified himself, and they could barely hear Bullard, as he left the living room.

Lacy looked over at Leia. "We could go sit outside again."

"It's too hot for me out there now. I'll go lie down for a

bit." With a wave of her fingers, she headed up to her bedroom.

Lacy looked over at the others. "It's nice that she trusts Bullard enough to make all this go away."

At that, Eton smiled. "I think, at this point in time, she knows that Bullard would go to the ends of the earth to keep her safe," he declared comfortably. "You will have that same reassurance, once you and Bojan get your crap together."

"Wouldn't that be nice," she muttered, stifling a sigh. "And yet … somehow, I think that process will take some time."

"Not all that much time, I don't think," Eton disagreed, looking over at her. "You guys have come a very long way already, so give him the ability to move a little closer, and I think you'll be fine."

She smiled. "I'm really glad telling you guys our story didn't result in everybody hating him or me."

"No, it all made us realize how precious the time we have with our loved ones really is and how lucky we are to have them in our lives," Eton shared. "I can't imagine everything you guys went through, and I don't even want to spend time or energy in that direction because it sounds horribly painful. The bottom line is that we're all doing what we can do, and hopefully you guys will find your way through."

Not a whole lot to say to that, but she agreed wholeheartedly. It was one of those scenarios where you hoped for the best, and meanwhile you kept on pushing forward and looking for answers.

When Bullard came back in a little bit later, his face was grim. "That's exactly what we have going on here. With his sister there for support, Charlie has been fully functioning.

He works for the delivery service. Apparently, after I fired him, Charlie had some sort of episodic break. He was on heavy medication, but then, on top of all that, losing his job with me, losing his mom, he was in a car accident and sustained more brain damage, and his condition worsened. He was under careful supervision with the sister, but she died unexpectedly after a stroke several days ago. The doctor knew that much, and the brother was supposed to go into a home, where his care could be managed, but he moved into an apartment with a friend instead and has become increasingly unstable. They've been looking for him so that they could get him back into a nursing home of some kind to be reevaluated."

"So, his mother's death probably started Charlie's downfall, but his sister's death was the incident that set him off, and, for whatever reason, he's blaming you, or maybe he was looking for something from you, didn't get it, and now he's spiraling," Lacy suggested.

"There's more," Bullard said. "Get this. The doc told me that Charlie's mom died. Of cancer. On the surgery table. Some ten years ago just after I fired him." Bullard levied a stare at Lacy.

Lacy nodded. "The medical file that Bojan chose, from among the victims of that killing doctor. That matches. And with their mom dead, that left the sister in charge of Charlie, with all his anger issues that then developed into psychological issues as well, maybe some drug interactions or addiction added to the mix."

"At least we know more about who and what we're dealing with now. We just have to find Charlie, and that wouldn't really be an issue, even without a damaged mind. However, someone with a damaged mind and extreme military experience may not be all that easy to bring in," Bullard pointed out.

"Maybe not, but that doesn't make it impossible either." Then Lacy stiffened, but immediately relaxed as Bojan walked in the front door. Dave and Ryland followed behind.

Bullard looked at her with a knowing expression. "You haven't had an easy time, but, since he's arrived and after yesterday, sometimes you seem better. Yet other times it seems to be grating on your nerves."

"It's not even that so much," she said, with a wry look, "but instead more about that feeling—when you reach out to give a big welcome to someone because you're so delighted to see them because they're so special in your world—and then you realize for the umpteenth time that you can't do that because, in their world, you're not special at all."

He shook his head. "You're wrong, Lacy. That's the way it *was*, not the way it is now. You've got to remember that, and you need to update your own memories."

And, with that, Bullard turned and walked out.

BOJAN WALKED IN with his senses already alert, knowing she wanted to remain in the living room with him. He studied her and, without giving her a chance to say a word, he walked over, leaned down, and gave her a powerful kiss. Whistling, he then headed to the kitchen, leaving her behind. He heard the laughter around them and her furious message in his head.

Did you have to do that?

No, I didn't have to, he replied, *but I really wanted to.*

At that came a stunned silence from her.

Yes, it's a whole new day, he said patiently. *It's a whole new world, and it will take us a bit of time to get there.*

Yeah, … well, it might take me a little longer than you.

We really don't have a whole lot of time to spend on adjusting, and it seems we've wasted enough already.

Well, that is hardly my fault, she snapped.

You're right. That's not your fault. It's mine, and I can't do anything more than apologize, but I won't spend the rest of our time hating what I did any more than I have to. So forgive me and get over it already. And, with that, he closed the door in his mind in her face.

Sometimes there was a great deal of joy in being able to close that door, and he was looking forward to the days when it wouldn't be necessary and when they would talk without pushing each other's buttons and setting them off. It's almost as if he wanted a warning sign on that door, before shit was about to hit the fan. Bojan was just glad that she and Leia were not in the room right now.

As it was, the team had far too little information on their shooter, but, as Bojan listened to Bullard bring them up to speed, it made a whole lot more sense. "So, it is directed at Leia," he noted, "though misdirected because our shooter doesn't understand that whatever happened between Bullard and his sister just happened." He frowned, yet with a nod.

"Well, I certainly don't have anything to be ashamed about," Bullard shared, standing in front of his men. "We didn't have much of a relationship to begin with, and, as I recall, she had somebody else in her life she wanted to be with." He spoke softly, his face thoughtful. "I'm not sure she ever told her brother about that because Charlie hated the guy."

"Well, that would be another reason for Charlie's confusion," Bojan added. "If his sister had hidden that relationship, then it's quite possible that Charlie wouldn't have seen his sister's growth in the relationship department."

"He wouldn't have taken it as being positive anyway," Bullard stated.

"The bottom line is," Bojan said, "we have to catch this guy before he does something to hurt anybody else, particularly Leia and Lacy, since he already hurt Lacy in lieu of Leia. As I see it, Charlie won't hold off until he gets the right person," Bojan winced. "He'll just shoot because I don't think his mind will be capable of sorting through all those details. Maybe before losing his sister he could have dealt with things better, but certainly not now."

"He'll continue to spiral out of control," Bullard agreed, "and that's bound to be bad news for us all."

"Absolutely," Bojan stated.

"So, on a more cheerful note, we get to keep the women locked inside, which makes security a bit easier," Bullard declared, looking around at the others, "Agreed?"

"*Humph*, you can say that," Bojan replied, almost choking, "but it won't happen."

"Well, if you don't tell Lacy, then it will be a surprise when Leia finds out," Bullard explained in a somewhat reasonable tone.

"Too late." Bojan gave Bullard a wry look. "I closed the door to my mind when I came in, knowing what kind of conversation we were likely to have, but Lacy opened it a minute ago, and I'm certain she just heard that."

Moments later, Lacy burst into the room, Leia on her heels, yet Lacy was fiery mad.

Knowing that he had to put a stop to it before it got out of control, Bojan got up, walked over, snatched her up into his arms, and laid the kiss of the century on her. When he lifted his head, Lacy sagged against him.

"That's hardly fair."

He looked over at the others to see them hiding smirks, but Leia was still glaring daggers at Bullard. Her gaze was on fire, and her tone could cut stones. "Are you trying to make me mad and my life even more stressful? You are not locking us up," she snapped. "And don't even think about trying Bojan's tactics on me," she muttered.

"Never." Bullard was too damn struck to say anything else.

"I'm not carrying your babies for nothing," she snapped. "But keeping us cooped up inside isn't healthy for any of us, mentally or physically. I've got two babies that don't need this added stress. It's your job to protect us, so you either do just that, or you tell me that you can't do it, in which case it's an entirely different situation," she muttered and continued to glare at her husband. "But it will be my decision on how I choose to handle it."

At that, Bullard rose beside her, glaring. "Don't ever imply that I can't look after you," he began, "but there is also a balance between keeping yourself safe and being foolish."

"Yes, asking us to stay indoors for a long period of time is a perfect example. The babies need fresh air, and we do too, and that's all there is to it."

"Babe, we need to make calculated decisions here."

"Find us a protected spot, even if you guys have to sit outside with sniper rifles at the ready," she snapped. "And, if you want to continue this discussion, believe me, I'm down for it. But this one? ... You *will* lose." And, with that, she poked him in the chest once and then again, as she added, "And, if you think you will take on a pregnant lady right now and start limiting the few enjoyable things she can do, especially sitting outside in the sun, then you better think again. *Your* babies need the peace and quiet found in Mother Nature." With another poke or two for good measure, she turned and walked out. "No wonder Lacy thinks I will deliver early," Leia muttered, and Bullard heard every word.

At that, Bojan looked over at Bullard and started to laugh. "Well, I guess you know where she stands," he muttered.

"Yeah, and I don't think you will get away with much else," Lacy added, yet still in Bojan's arms. "Keeping us inside is a bad idea. And she's right. We both prefer to be outside in the sunshine, so, if you can't find a way to protect us out there, then something is wrong here. This may be deemed your home, but it is an enclosed compound, and, yes, I know you're already fixing the security on the back side. So we'll give you until tomorrow to have that fixed," she declared in an ominous tone.

"How kind of you." Bullard's tone was biting.

"As Leia suggested, you may need somebody out there with sniper rifles to address any threat," she muttered. "Surely this guy doesn't have equipment beyond that."

"Don't be so sure," Bullard corrected. "This guy could have access to the same type of equipment that we do."

Lacy sighed. "You better find him fast because you sure don't want to tell Leia that she can't go outside. I already know what that answer will be. I'm not looking forward to the fact that I have to tell her that I gave you until tomorrow."

He rolled his eyes. "Nothing scarier than a pregnant woman."

"Yeah, there is," Lacy argued. "A pregnant woman almost to term who's carrying twins. Don't bring out the warrior within—or the mama bear either. She and those babies don't need the added stress at this time."

THE REST OF the day Bojan watched as Bullard pulled every string in the book to try and set up the further enhanced security outside—both of the high-tech variety as well as extra manpower—even as he moved forward at top speed on the security efforts on the adjacent property he'd just purchased. Having Leia confront him made him face the fact that this would happen on her timetable, not his, and he needed to get after it, if he wanted to keep up with his very pregnant wife.

He had absolutely no doubt that life would get very difficult for all of them if they didn't find the shooter really soon. They had already tracked down everything they could as far as bullets. The police had been brought in because of the deceased body found at Charlie's apartment. That body had been identified as a long-term friend, who had been receiving treatment in the same therapy group. It was still undetermined whether the guy had committed suicide or had been murdered. The police weren't talking, but having seen the scenario himself, Bojan was pretty darn sure murder was on the table. Which meant that this Charlie guy probably had a very short fuse and even now was looking for a way to get back at Bullard.

As Bullard walked into the huge dining room—where Bojan was working on a laptop, trying to track other places the shooter was known to haunt—Bullard dropped a folder on the table and announced, "Well, I know *why now* at least."

"You do?" Bojan asked.

"Yeah, apparently the car accident took him back in time. Like seriously regressed his brain back almost two decades, to when I was going out with his sister, and Charlie's memories stopped there. So, it has nothing to do with my behavior, her behavior, or anything else, but in his brain? … It's still some fifteen years ago, and he hasn't been able to let it go that his sister and I broke up. And it was his sister's idea."

At that, Bojan nodded slowly. "That makes more sense. … While my heart goes out to the guy, we still have to stop him."

"Yeah, you're not kidding." Bullard glared down at the paperwork spread around him. "The doctor didn't have any ideas where Charlie would go or who he hangs out with, except that he'd made a bunch of friends through his therapy group. It required some arm twisting, but the doc has just given us that list."

"Good." Bojan hopped up. "I can't stand sitting around, so I'll grab a bunch of those names and go."

"I'm coming with you," Ryland said.

"Twelve names are here," Bullard pointed out, "so split them up. Get two or three teams out, and let's cover them as quickly as possible. We need to find Charlie and fast. Meanwhile, this place is on full lockdown, so make sure you use full security measures coming and going. I don't need to tell you how bad things can get."

Within a matter of minutes, the three teams were gathered. Ryland grabbed the list and quickly divided the names among the groups. "We need addresses, and we don't have them," he muttered.

Bullard nodded. "Yeah, the doctor wouldn't give me addresses for these guys, due to privacy legalities," he noted, with an eye roll, "but I've already called the cops, and the ones they found right away are printing now. Just give me a minute."

"Will the cops be okay if we go look for these people?" Bojan asked.

"They're pretty short on manpower. They said they'll be on their way, but it won't be anytime soon. Therefore, we have to share whatever information we have. So, yeah, we can take a look first."

"Works for me," Bojan replied. "It's better to have the local authorities on our side anyway. If we get there and get the legwork done before them, we're still better off."

"Exactly, so get loaded up and go. Here are the addresses we have. I will forward the others, as soon as I get them."

And, with that, the three teams headed out. As soon as Bojan and Ryland hopped into their vehicle, Ryland spoke up. "Is there a reason why you grabbed these particular names?"

"Yeah. I remembered them from some of the background info we had on Charlie. At least two of the names here stand out. He worked with one of these guys at a previous job, and I figured he had a closer connection than others may to Charlie."

"That would make sense." Ryland nodded. "Let's get after it."

"Glad to see you guys don't waste time."

"No, we sure don't," Ryland confirmed. "Did you get any readings off the list?"

"Yeah, I did, and now my bet's on this guy"—Bojan pointed at a name on their list—"but still something's off about it."

"*Great*," Ryland muttered, staring at him for a moment. "Are we talking about a dead body kind of *off*, like last time?"

"Possibly," he replied. "I don't know what to say to that until we get there, and there's absolutely no way to know."

"Got it," Ryland said.

"You want to go there first?"

"Yes."

And that's what they did. It was a small apartment on the lower level of a four-story apartment building. It appeared a little rough, but that was to be expected because they were in a low-income area. As Bojan got out of the vehicle, he studied the grimy walls and the dusty windows. "I guess this is the kind of place where Charlie would hide out, right?"

"Maybe," Ryland said, "but you can't ever count on that. Fortunes rise and fall."

"Yeah, but don't you often see those who are rising then sometimes fall again right afterward, as if they got money in, then it went right back out again?"

"Usually, especially when drugs are involved, you know?"

"Yep, we just can't make that assumption yet."

Agreeing with that, Ryland headed to the doorway of the first address, then looked down at the paperwork in his hand and asked, "So this is the guy named Ripper?"

"What kind of a name is *Ripper*?" Bojan asked.

"It's a name he legally changed to, but it's not Ripper. It's *Rippa*," Ryland clarified.

"I kinda prefer that pronunciation," Bojan quipped.

With a chuckle, they knocked on the door and waited

but got no answer. Putting an ear to the door, Ryland looked over at Bojan and shrugged. "I don't know about you, but I don't have a problem walking in and checking to ensure this guy is okay, since the previous guy was dead."

"Works for me," Bojan agreed. "Besides, you have a better handle on what you can get by with here than I do."

"What I can get away with and what Bullard can get away with are two different things," he noted cheerfully, as he quickly picked the lock, pushed the door open, and called out, "Rippa? Anybody home?"

There was no answer. They walked to the far side and quickly scanned the apartment but found no sign of anyone. Frowning, they stepped back outside, locked up the door.

"I didn't see anything, did you?" Bojan asked Ryland.

"No, not at all, plus there was no paperwork, no mail, or anything like that. It's almost like it wasn't even lived in, or, if it was, it wasn't a full-time location."

At that, Bojan thought for a moment. "In a way that kind of makes sense. Maybe this guy's got a girlfriend or something, but his money pays for this much."

"I don't know how that works, but, if he's got disability payments or something that's covering the cost of an apartment, then he'll keep this regardless. The last thing he wants to do is lose that kind of government money. But you would think that they would move in here."

"Right," Bojan agreed. "He could also be in the hospital for treatment or something."

"Yeah, I hadn't considered that. These guys are probably frequent flyers. Maybe run a check and see." They quickly ran the name through a hospital records program and found a match. "Bingo."

Bojan stared at the data brought up in front of him and

swore. "He was admitted for an overdose yesterday."

At that, Ryland looked at him, frowned, and suggested, "Better call the hospital and see if we can get in to talk to him."

"Will do," Bojan confirmed. "Meanwhile, let's keep driving and head to the second location." Ryland drove toward the second address, while Bojan was still on hold with the hospital. When he finally got through, he was informed that the patient was allowed visitors, but only with supervised visitation, and they must have permission.

"How do we get permission?" he asked the nurse. By the time he got the doctor's name, so he could request permission, he had everything written down and shook his head. "I wonder if we need to bring in the cops on this one."

"Maybe," Ryland said, "but Bullard can also talk to the doctor, if it's one he knows, and maybe get us permission to get in." Bojan quickly sent a text to Bullard, then, when the vehicle stopped at their second address, Bojan hopped out, and the two of them walked up to the target door. When they knocked, the door was answered by a woman with frizzy red hair sticking out all over. She had wild-looking eyes, wore an artist's smock, and was covered in paint.

"What do you want?" she yelled. "Jesus, why can't people ever just leave me alone?"

Bojan stepped forward with a gentle smile. "I'm so sorry to bother you, ma'am," he began politely. "I didn't realize you were painting."

"Of course I'm painting. I'm always painting. What do you want?" She looked at him suspiciously.

"We're trying to find a friend of yours," he replied, then he gave her Charlie's name.

She shook her head. "I haven't seen him. Why the hell

do other guys have to keep coming around here?" *Other guys* stood out in the whole sentence, but Bojan watched her as she went off. "I haven't seen him in a long time. Not since he went kind of strange."

Bojan wasn't sure what *strange* would mean to somebody who was already looking like the queen of strange herself, but he asked in a quiet voice, "Could you explain what you mean by that?"

"He went loco. I mean, his medication even had to be changed. He seemed to be getting really delusional. He had this thing about some guy named Bullward, Ballad, something like that. I don't know if it was a man or an animal or a song, not the way Charlie was talking. It was pretty damn hard to tell, but he wanted to make him pay."

"Well, that's why we're trying to find Charlie. He is attempting to hurt this man and his pregnant wife."

At that, her eyebrows shot up. "That's not good," she muttered, trying to shut the door. "Look. I've got nothing to do with it. I don't know anything about it, and I don't want to deal with this mess," she bellowed. "Charlie's really kind of scary. I only knew him through our group sessions, and, even then, I didn't get very friendly."

"That's probably a good thing," Bojan shared, trying not to spook her, but it was hard not to. "If you do hear from him—"

She shook her head. "As I said, he hasn't been here in a very long time, so I'm sure he won't contact me when he runs into trouble," she muttered.

"Are you sure about that because it sounded as if you guys were friends."

"At one time we were friends." She sniffed the air. "Then he started insulting my art and just generally … being an ass." As she spoke, she was closing the door again some-what. "I had enough of it very quickly. Everything in his life was about his sister. Even she couldn't keep him under control. As I told you already, it started to get really weird."

"Do you know where we might find him?" Bojan asked quickly, before she totally shut the door in their faces. "It's really important that we find him before he hurts somebody else."

"Somebody else?" She picked up on that immediately, her gaze narrowing at him.

"Yes, somebody else," Bojan repeated.

She sighed. "I'm not sure. He used to hang around at the pool halls to drink and at the wildlife rescue centers because he likes working with animals, but I know he got kicked out of there at one point in time."

"What about other friends?"

"Sally," she said. "They were doing a lot of drinking, and I hate to say drugs, but I do think they were into doing drugs together," she shared reluctantly. "It's not allowed in our sessions. Well, it's not allowed period. We're on so much medication already, and adding drugs can really compli-cate …" She stopped her babble and shrugged. "Not everybody wants to fix their lives."

"Agreed. So how do we find Sally?"

"Two buildings over from the one Charlie lived in," she said, closing her eyes and pondering for a moment. "Ground floor, first apartment from the left, but I don't remember the number."

"Does this Sally have a last name?" Bojan asked.

She hesitated for a moment, then shrugged. "She must, but I'm not sure I ever heard one."

"Good enough."

She slammed the door in his face then, not giving him a chance to ask anything else. He turned and looked over at Ryland, who was already on his phone. "There was a Sally on one of the lists," he confirmed, giving him a look. "It's not in our names though."

"Well, let's head there anyway."

"Yeah, I just want to make sure that the team going there gets a heads-up."

"We'll meet them there, if they're already on the way. If they haven't got that far, they can take it off their list, and we'll hit it up."

By the time they got to the right address, they still had no update on getting permission to see Rippa in the hospital.

When they walked up to the building, a woman was coming out. Bojan quickly walked forward and helped her with the door, which conveniently let them in as well. She thanked him, and he said, "I'm looking for Sally, but I don't know if she's home. Have you seen her lately?"

"Sally, oh my," she replied, with a laugh. "Sally is always here. That place is a hub of activity." He looked over to the first door on the left, and she nodded. "Yeah, so if you were expecting anything more than that, be prepared. She got clientele there fairly regularly."

"What kind of clientele?" he asked, already hating the wince in his voice.

She burst out laughing. "I'm sure you can imagine, and, if the two of you were looking for something special, she can probably accommodate you. Me, on the other hand, I like one at a time. I prefer to keep them separate." She shook her head. "Sally doesn't appear to care."

"Ah, well, I'm not here for her services or as a friend."

"Yeah, you sure?" She studied the two men and

shrugged. "No, you're not her type, are you? Too clean-cut and you both look like you've got your acts together. Not so much for the guys she's usually got hanging around that place."

He quickly pulled out a picture of Charlie and held it up for her. "Have you seen this one here?"

She looked at it and frowned. "Yeah, a couple times, but I don't know that I've seen him lately. Why, is he in trouble?"

"Yeah, loads of it," Bojan replied. "So, if you do see him, best to stay away."

She froze and asked, "Seriously?"

He nodded. "Yes, and there could be cops around here soon."

She groaned. "In that case, maybe I'll go visit my mom for the rest of the day. Make sure you guys pick him up before I get home, will you? I mean, this is a tough enough place to live without dealing with that kind of riffraff."

"This Sally, do you know anything about her?"

"She's a good-time girl," she replied, bringing her smile back out, "generally harmless, so I don't have any argument with her, as long she keeps the noise down. Live and let live, as far as I'm concerned. She's not hurting anybody, or she wasn't anyway." She looked at him cautiously. "But, if she was involved, that would surprise me."

"As far as we know she's not, but we still need to investigate further."

"Of course you do," she muttered. "Law enforcement, *huh*?"

It was Ryland who stepped in and clarified, "*Private*."

"Of course you're private. Everything around here is private, at least if you want to get anything done." She sighed. "Okay, just give me ten minutes, and I'm out of here." And, with that, she quickly walked back into her apartment.

Ryland looked over at Bojan. "Let's go check out Sally's place." They headed across to the apartment in question. Ryland looked at him. "Do we want to give her a chance to get out of here first?"

Bojan shrugged. "At the moment it's quiet, so with any luck we'll be talking to Sally while the other neighbor lady gets out to visit her mom. I don't know how long we have before the cops get here, and, if Charlie were to make a run out the back, I sure wouldn't want it to be in that ten-minute window."

Ryland nodded. "In that case, let's go."

They stepped up to the door and knocked. When a shout came from the other side, they waited.

Then a woman's face appeared in the crack behind the chain holding the door partially open. She stared at them. "I don't know you guys," she stated abruptly, and there was no party-girl fun in her expression at all.

"No," Bojan confirmed, "we've never met."

"So why are you here?"

He looked at her and saw the tears and the puffy cheeks. "Well, we're looking for Charlie. Is he in there?"

Her eyes widened with fear and she shifted to look around behind them, then she shook her head. "No, he isn't." Then she looked at them miserably. "How did you know?" she asked in a hoarse whisper.

"Let me guess. He's gone kind of crazy, a little bit out of control, not the same as he used to be?"

Her eyes widened with every statement, and she nodded slowly. "But I don't understand how," she cried out. "I didn't tell anyone. I told him that I wouldn't tell, and I didn't, but he will blame me now." Then she started to sob.

At that, Bojan looked over at Ryland, who just shrugged and looked at her. "May we come in?" he asked. She hesitated but then unhooked the chain and opened it up for them. When they stepped inside, Bojan watched as the other woman quickly exited her apartment, locking her door and heading toward the exit. He turned to look at Sally, who wore just a robe. Her cheeks were red, puffy, and tear-stained, with streaks of mascara. Visible bruises were all over her as well. "When did he do that to you?"

Sally shrugged. "This isn't anything." She sniffled and wiped away at her nose. "At least not compared to everything else he's done. It's just … nothing."

"It's all gotten much worse over the last couple weeks since his sister died, right?"

She looked at him, blinked, and asked, "Is that what set him off, his sister?"

Bojan nodded. "She died about ten days ago."

"Jesus, why wouldn't he tell me then? I kept asking him what I'd done, what was wrong, but he wouldn't tell me."

"I'm not sure he's capable of knowing at the moment. He's too enraged."

"Oh, he's enraged all right," she muttered. "He's furious."

At that, he looked at her and asked, "Where is he right now?"

"I don't know. He took off this morning in a huff and hasn't come back yet. If he comes back and finds you here, you'll set him off again." She groaned. "You guys need to leave and don't come back." She got up and walked to the door with an air of determination. She flung it open and declared, "You need to leave right now."

"Why? In case he comes back?"

"Yeah. You don't know him like I do. He will …" Then she stopped and started to cry. "He will beat me up again, and I just don't think I can handle that."

"You shouldn't have to," Bojan told her. "He's out of control, and he needs help."

She looked at him and sobbed. "Nobody can help him. He's really a good guy, or at least he can be. But now? … Now he's just messed up."

"He is messed up, and, when he's messed up, he needs help," Bojan told her, "but, in this case, the trouble's gotten pretty bad."

She stared at him, shaking her head. "He didn't mean to hurt me though, and he always says he's sorry."

"Of course he did. Do you believe him?"

"Of course. I know he means it," she replied, her tone sincere. "I just don't know how to help him."

"You can't help him, Sally. He's also made threats and shot at other people."

At that, her gaze widened. "Oh, no, he's not supposed to take that gun anywhere."

"He has a gun?" Ryland asked. "What is it? Do you know where it is?"

"It's two numbers together, a .22 or something."

"Or a .44," Bojan corrected in a dry tone.

She flicked a glance his way and then nodded. "That might have been it," she admitted grudgingly. "I don't even know where he got it. He just appeared with it one day."

"Appearing with it is one thing, but using it is another."

"Well, he's never shot me," she stated, as if that explained everything.

Bojan sighed. "Look. I'm sorry. This is obviously distressing to you, but he has threatened some people with that gun, and we need to make sure he doesn't hurt them again."

"You mean, like me?" she muttered.

"The woman he's threatening to hurt is eight months pregnant, and we don't want anything to happen to her or to the babies."

Her gaze widened at that. "He would never hurt a pregnant woman. No way."

"He's hurting you."

"But he doesn't mean to," she argued.

Bojan didn't say anything to that because there wasn't anything he could say to change her mind. People who were beaten up and abused often made excuses for their abuser, and it was pretty hard for them to see that the accused really wasn't the sympathetic, caring person they were staying for. However, that brainwashing went deep, and it wasn't something Bojan could fix in one short conversation. He looked over at Ryland, then asked her, "Do you have any idea where he is right now?"

She shook her head. "No, I don't."

"As soon as you come up with a place or places we can go check, then we can leave, hopefully before he does come home," Bojan stated.

"You'll leave?" she asked eagerly.

"Sure," he agreed, looking at her curiously. "We don't want to see you get hurt even more."

"He won't hurt me again," she said, and then she sniffled past her tears and rubbed her eyes, smearing mascara on the back of her hand, which she didn't even notice.

"Does he have any favorite haunts or places he likes to go? Does he go shopping anywhere? Do you know why he went out?"

"He was angry. He wanted to go teach somebody a lesson, but I don't know who he wanted to go see. He used to go see his sister all the time, but, if she died, well, … I guess that's when he got all messed up."

"Did he ever hurt his sister?" Bojan asked curiously.

"No, he used to go over there all the time because he loved her."

"Well, love's important."

She smiled and nodded. "He loves me too."

Bojan didn't say anything to that, just asked again, "So, where would he have gone?"

When she remained silent, Ryland added, "Is there a park he goes to? Someplace he goes for a walk? Where?"

"I don't know," she replied nervously. "I just don't."

Bojan assessed her energy for a long moment, then realized that she did have some ideas but didn't know for sure.

"How about some guesses?" he asked. "Just give us something to check out, somewhere we might find him, before he hurts somebody. We really don't want anyone to think you're a part of this, so you need to cooperate."

Her gaze widened. "I'm not a part of it," she cried out in horror.

"Yet, if you don't help and if you did know where he went, you would be considered an accomplice, and more so, even charged as one," he reminded her.

She shook her head. "I don't know. I really don't know."

"Okay, good enough. Did he have to go get groceries? Where would he have gone and done some shopping for ammo or anything like that?"

She looked up and then something came into her mind. "He wanted to see somebody else the other day. He said that sometimes, when he's angry, he likes to think about stopping in and seeing old friends."

"Do you remember who though?"

She shook her head. "No, but I know one of his friends is in hospital."

"Yeah, did he know anything about that? Did he mention it?"

"No, he just mentioned that it was really bad and that life isn't the same as it used to be."

"Did he hurt that friend of his?"

"I don't think so. He was just pretty upset about it. They would go do something together, and then I think this other guy got upset and maybe chickened out."

"That could be," he murmured. Then he mentioned the man whose body they found. "Do you know him?"

She nodded. "Yeah, I do. We'd been in therapy a couple times, at least some of our group sessions," she muttered. "He's a good guy."

"Yeah, and what about your boyfriend, did he know him?"

She nodded. "Yeah, he did. We're all from the same group. We're all friends." She said *friends*, as if having friends was a badge of honor.

He nodded. "Did you know he's dead?"

She looked at him, and her bottom lip trembled. She shook her head. "No, I didn't know."

"He was shot," Bojan explained, trying to ease the blow that was coming, "with a .44."

She stared at him, and her bottom lip started to wobble. "Did Charlie do it?" she whispered.

"I don't know, but that's one of the questions we need to ask him," Bojan told her. "Because we can't have him going around killing people. We do know that he's threatened this pregnant woman, and we're trying to keep her safe too."

At that, Sally stared at him, clearly on information overload.

Honestly, Bojan felt badly for her, but he didn't know any other way to get information out of her.

She just shook her head. "I don't know. I don't know anything," she wailed. "He wouldn't do something like that."

"I hope not," Bojan said. "But you're one of his friends, and he's already got friends in both the morgue and the hospital. He has already made a habit of beating you up, so you might want to keep that in mind the next time he comes around, looking to use you as a punching bag."

She looked at him. "He won't hurt me."

"He already has," he reminded her.

But she shook her head and glared at him. "He didn't mean to."

"I'm glad to hear that," Bojan said, "because, if he ever *means* to, I rather imagine he'll kill you."

CHAPTER 10

L ACY CHECKED IN on Leia a little bit later and found her sitting upstairs on her deck with a book. "Ready for a cup of tea?"

"Maybe. It's either that or a divorce." Leia groaned.

At that, Lacy burst out laughing.

"I suppose you think it's funny," Leia grumbled, with a weak smile.

"As you and I both know, nothing is quite like pregnant women when dealing with problems blowing up in your face."

"No kidding." Leia sighed. "I probably should apologize, but, at the same time, I don't really want to."

Lacy grinned at her. "I understand the sentiment. Everybody also understands how you're feeling, and it's really not a big deal right now," she murmured.

"No, but I still feel guilty."

"Of course you do. But they will fix this, one way or another. I know that right now we have multiple teams out looking for this shooter." Then she went on to explain the little bits she had heard through the grapevine.

At that, Leia nodded. "Bullard did fill me in on the progress they've made," she acknowledged, "so I know that they're on it. It's just frustrating. I really just wanted this time to peacefully nest. Instead we have all this strife and fear, which is the last thing my babies and I need."

"Right, you've been through enough of that already," Lacy stated. "So put your faith in Bullard and the team. Chill out, relax, and don't get upset about it. We are getting it solved."

Leia smiled at her. "I was wondering about going for a swim. What do you think?"

"I think you should," she agreed, "and I'll come with you."

"Why? To keep an eye on me?" she joked.

"Partially, yes," she admitted. "I would hate to see you fall or get into trouble with that belly of yours right now. Other than that, I'm always first in the pool."

"You really do enjoy it, don't you?"

"Yes, I would love to be at a lake or on the ocean, but a pool still gives you that extra few months to swim during the summer season. I thoroughly enjoy a chance to relax, and it helps me to destress."

"Okay, that's it then. Let's head to the pool. Maybe we'll take a pitcher of lemonade or something out with us."

"Sounds good," Lacy agreed.

As she went to leave, Leia called out, "Do you know where the men are now?"

She turned to face Leia. "All over the place. Why? Did you want anybody in particular?"

"No, I just wondered if you've picked up anything from Bojan."

"I know that he's going from house to house, checking out where our shooter might be holed up, and that's apparently been a bit of a problem. Charlie was last seen this morning, when he left his girlfriend's place after beating her up in a temper fit."

At that, Leia stared at her. "Would you … You would tell me if this guy was on his way, right?"

Lacy nodded. "If I knew, I would tell you," she declared, trying to appear calm and to ignore the fear setting in, "but there is no guarantee I would know. My visions are kind of hit and miss. Sometimes they don't make sense, until in hindsight."

Leia's shoulders slumped. "Right, there are never answers when you want them."

"Well, there are always answers, but we can't just pull them out of a hat whenever we want to. Just because we want answers doesn't mean we get them."

"Of course not," Leia muttered, followed by half a sigh.

"What we're really trying to figure out is where Charlie will go from there, and that's not our problem. It's theirs," she stated.

Leia laughed, trying to discard her worry. "Fine, I'll get changed and come down."

"Do you want me to wait up here for you?"

Leia frowned at her in surprise. "Are you going to get changed?"

"I am."

"Go get changed then and come back here," she suggested.

And, with that, the two women split up. Lacy raced to her room, called Dave to give him the heads-up on their location change, then quickly put on her bathing suit, grabbed a coverup for when she was out in the sun, and then walked back over to Leia. "You're getting around pretty well, considering how chunky you are," Lacy teased, with a chuckle.

"*Chunky*. … That is one way to put it," Leia muttered.

"I've spent a lot of time dealing with pregnancies, and I've seen an awful lot of big bellies, but it's different when it's not your own, and you don't have that same experience."

"Absolutely," Lacy confirmed, with a smile. "But now you're the pregnant one, and it's something you've always wanted. It's a gift, so let's enjoy every moment."

She laughed. "Well, *you* can enjoy every moment of it. … You're not pregnant." Then she shot Lacy a look. "You're not, are you?"

At that, Lacy shook her head. "Definitely not pregnant."

"I don't know whether I should say sorry or congratulations."

Lacy burst out laughing. "It's all good, so, if and when I ever get there, hopefully I will enjoy the process. But, until then, it's really not the right time."

"It will be though," Leia said. "You guys are doing so much better."

"We just need some time now," she noted.

"That's right. Time to yourselves and time to sort out all that has happened in your lives. It's incredible to think about what you've already been through."

Lacy snorted. "Not so much, and, if you put it on the scale, compared to what other people have experienced, it's not much at all. You've been through an awful lot more. It just looks different when it's not our own life. I mean, we lived it, so it becomes almost normal. Yet, to other people, it seems pretty crazy."

At the pool, the two women carefully made their way into the water, and, while Leia did a bit of floating, Lacy swam. By the time she had worked out some of the kinks in her shoulders, she was more than ready to come out.

Leia was still sitting in the shallow end of the pool,

watching Lacy.

When Lacy came up for the last time, she smiled at Leia and asked, "Are you ready to get out?"

Leia gave her a tired nod. "I wasn't sure I could make it out of here on my own, though," she admitted.

"You should have stopped me earlier," Lacy scolded. "I wouldn't have minded at all."

"But you were doing so well," Leia pointed out. "And that at least made me feel good, living vicariously through you, as you swam like the fish you are. I swim very well myself, just not when I'm the size of a whale."

All the size jokes were fun and games, but still they made Lacy worry that Leia was really struggling with her pregnancy. "You're really okay to be in this condition, aren't you?"

"Absolutely," Leia declared, looking straight at Lacy. "I know I joke about it, but there's really not an upside to being this size and shape. I'm spending half my day running to the bathroom. I haven't seen my toes in months and can't put on my shoes without Bullard's help," she noted with laugh, "but I wouldn't change it for the world."

"Good, you had me worried there for a minute."

"No, no concerns at all. Except I'm really wishing we had brought some lemonade out with us."

"I agree, and I can go get it. I don't know how many people are inside, but I sure don't want to start calling people to haul stuff out here."

"That's exactly what Bullard would expect you to do."

"He can expect what he likes, but I'm still freely independent," Lacy muttered. She looked around at the far side of the compound where the wall and trees were. "I don't even know if anybody is out there or not."

"You would hope so, at least as far as the good guys are

concerned, but it's hard to say," Leia muttered. "As long as nobody bothers us, I'm good."

"Well, he did buy that extra swath of land to please you," Lacy said.

"You mean to please himself," she corrected, with a big laugh. "He's been talking about buying that property forever. This just gave him a good excuse to do so."

After retrieving the lemonade, the two of them relaxed, with the icy-cold pitcher between them, as they napped, read books, and generally relaxed.

Lacy sat up with a jolt as a voice slammed into her head. She started looking around for Bojan. "Bojan, are you here?" she asked, certain that she heard someone calling out loud. When Leia looked over at her, Lacy frowned, got up, and explained, "I thought I heard something."

"Sounded like you thought you heard Bojan," Leia said in a teasing voice. "Right? You would think that that would be something there would be no doubt about."

Lacy sent out another call to Bojan, this time in her head, and he responded back, frustrated and impatient, and Lacy realized it wasn't him calling for her. "Sorry, I thought you called me," she replied, then quickly closed the door between them. She looked around, wondering what the devil she'd heard. She walked into the kitchen, and Pia was there working away on dinner. Lacy then walked into the dining room and found it was empty. Bullard was on the phone in his office, and there was a general sense of activity. At least here. With teams out looking for Charlie, there was a general sense that the property was largely empty.

Suddenly she worried that this guy might have found a way to enter the compound and was even now inside the walls, while the teams were searching for him on the outside.

She quickly hurried back to Leia, not wanting to leave her alone. As she stepped outside, Leia looked at her, terrified, while a man held a gun to her head. Lacy froze and then carefully walked toward him. "Hey, Charlie," she greeted him, with a gentle smile.

He looked up at her and glared, almost terrified, yet furious. "I killed you," he snarled.

She nodded. "You did, but I'm back," she murmured. "So I'm sorry if you think that killing me gets rid of the ghosts in your life, but it doesn't. It just makes us angry."

He waved the gun in her direction, and thankfully it was now away from Leia's head.

Lacy immediately started slamming out requests to Bojan and Terkel to notify Bullard that they were in trouble. She even reached out to Pia and slammed a message into his brain, but, whether he got it or not, she wasn't sure. She walked closer to Charlie, and he pointed the gun at her.

"I'll kill you again," he spat.

She shrugged. "You can try, but I'm already dead. What's the point of wasting the bullet?"

He blinked a few times, staring at her.

"Did you take your medicine today? Your sister says that you're supposed to take your medicine all the time, right?"

He shook his head. "You're not my sister."

"No, I'm not your sister, but she's here with you. You know that, right? I mean, think about it. If I'm here, then surely she's got to be here, especially since she loves you so much."

He shook his head. "No, she's not here. She's dead."

"Yeah, well, you already shot me dead, and I'm here," Lacy argued, "so what makes you think your sister's not here too?" She knew this talk would confuse the man and was hoping that would buy her some time. She continued to walk around the pool, as he watched her with glaring eyes. "Why would you want to hurt Leia?" Lacy asked. "She's done nothing to you."

"Because of Bullard," he roared, the gun turning back toward Leia again.

Lacy reached out with her mind and pushed at the air around Leia, trying to create a protective bubble around her. It would probably be easier to shift the air in front of the actual gun muzzle itself, but Charlie kept moving it erratically, and that made it hard for her to keep her energy stable.

Bojan slammed into her brain, asking what was going on.

She gave him a disjointed version, but added, *We're in trouble. The gunman's here.*

On our way.

"Yeah, too late," she murmured, and then she refocused on Charlie. "Your sister loved you. She loved you to bits. She didn't love Bullard. She loved her boyfriend."

Charlie's face twisted with fury. "I told her that he was no good, that she knew better."

"She might have known better, but, when you love somebody, it doesn't matter whether you know better or not," Lacy replied. "It's definitely not something you can control all the time."

"That's not true," he cried out. "She loved Bullard."

"No, she didn't. She's the one who broke it off." She wasn't exactly sure how that had worked but knew that Bullard believed something along that line.

"It doesn't matter," Charlie snapped. "She was with Bullard, so he should have looked after her."

"Ah, you mean, if Bullard had looked after her, she

wouldn't have gotten sick? Is that it?" she asked, her voice soft. "That kind of makes sense in a way."

He nodded. "Exactly." Charlie waved the gun between Lacy and Leia. "So it's his fault. You see that, right?"

"Well, it's not his fault, but you're looking for somebody to blame, so he'll do nicely, I gather." She looked down at Leia to see the fear and terror in her eyes. In the distance overhead she saw somebody in the trees, but he wasn't moving, and now she was worried Charlie had hired a backup to stand out there as well.

She looked back at him. "How many people have you hurt, trying to make Bullard pay for something he didn't do?" she asked him. "Did you hurt this other man too?"

He just stared at her. "Didn't hurt him. I just knocked him out."

"So, knocking him out didn't hurt him?" she asked curiously, wondering just how damaged Charlie's mind was.

"No, it didn't hurt him." Charlie shrugged. "But, if it did, too bad!"

"Too bad, *huh*? I'm not sure there's any brain damage at all when I look at you," she shared, keeping her focus on him. "Everything outside seems just fine. You're just angry because things didn't happen the way you wanted them to. Was it because of your sister loving another man or because your sister got sick?" she murmured. "But you know full well that Bullard didn't have anything to do with it."

"Bullard is responsible," he yelled, using the gun for emphasis on certain words. "No way he isn't," he muttered. "I'll make him pay. He took my sister from me, so I'll take his love from him."

"Oh, well, that would be me," Lacy declared. "But you already killed me, remember?" He looked so confused for a moment that she almost felt sorry for him. But, at the same time, Lacy was busy rolling the energy up around Leia, hoping desperately that she could protect her friend from a bullet. Lacy wasn't sure that was even possible, but she was hoping so. By the time Charlie figured it out, it would be too late, and somebody else would be out here to help. Unfortunately, Charlie wasn't buying her version of events.

"Bullard is to blame!" he roared.

At that, the door behind him slammed open, and Bullard himself stepped out. "Charlie, if I'm to blame, why the hell aren't you trying to shoot me then?" His own bullish roar made the air split with his fury. "How dare you come back after my wife."

Charlie looked at him and almost cringed. The gun came up with the same bravado, as he glared at him. "It's your fault!" he roared. "She's dead because of you."

"I did not cause her heart to have a stroke," Bullard yelled back, and then his voice softened. "Jesus, man, we were friends."

"Until you killed my sister."

Bullard just looked at him, as if trying to figure out how to get through to Charlie.

Lacy sent a probe out, trying to see if she could get inside his brain, but everything there didn't seem to fit properly. She couldn't see the damage on the outside, but, on the inside, it was way worse. "What happened to your head?" she asked. He looked at her, then back at Bullard and didn't say anything. "It was a war wound?"

"Originally, yes. But then there was a car accident," he admitted reluctantly. "They said I would never be back to normal."

"That's not very fair, is it?"

He shrugged. "It doesn't matter. Without my sister, it doesn't matter at all."

It was obvious that the grief was overtaking him, as he began to sob. Bullard took several steps toward him, but the gun came up once again.

"No, you don't," Charlie yelled. "You're not getting out of this one."

"I don't care what you do to me," Bullard said desperately, "but I don't want you hurting Leia."

"I didn't want you hurting my sister either," Charlie snarled. "That didn't matter to you, did it?"

There really was no helping a broken mind, and Lacy knew that. However, she'd been hoping to avoid any kind of massive argument. It was obvious from Charlie's reaction that he wanted blood, and it must be Leia's blood to make him happy. Lacy looked down at Leia and smiled at her reassuringly. She looked back toward the house to see Pia staring out, watching in shock, his phone to his ear. Bojan was in the back of her head, telling her to hold on, that he was almost there. She was telling him to go to the back of the property. That's where she could see somebody half in and half out of the tree, maybe Charlie's accomplice.

He barked back, inside her mind. *I don't give a damn about the tree or whoever is in it. You hold on.*

"Doesn't matter. I'm already good as dead," she muttered calmly.

At Bojan's shock, she almost smiled. She looked over at the gunman and sent a wave of loving energy toward Charlie, but it came up against nothing but cold darkness. She frowned at that because it wasn't something she was used to feeling, certainly not when it came to using her energy in hospital settings. Most times, when working on healing somebody, she found at least a level of receptivity that she could work with. Yet, in this case, it seemed like everything was blocked; everything was locked down tight.

She tried again and went with a little bit of energy inside his body but again found nothing. It seemed the receptors themselves were damaged. With horror, she realized that there might be nothing she could do beyond doing her best to try and protect Leia. She had really hoped she could do something to help Charlie's broken mind, but instead the broken mind sent out such fury and hate that she realized some things just could not be fixed, and this appeared to be one of them.

BOJAN AND RYLAND drove around to the back of the property. Then they quickly bolted from the vehicle and headed toward the huge dividing wall on the east side. All the while, checking to see if the security system was on, Bojan realized that it wasn't. He held up a hand signal for Ryland and asked, "Why is this not on?"

Ryland shook his head. "Probably because we're in the middle of fixing it," he muttered. "Of course this Charlie guy either has the luck of the devil, or he brought it down himself, or knew how to bypass it all."

"It could be anything," Bojan agreed, "but what are the chances that, when he delivered that parcel, he also put a listening device inside?"

"I don't know. He would have just handed his delivery to somebody on the inside, right?"

"Did anybody check that picture to see if there was any-thing on it?"

Ryland shot him a look. "I don't know, but that's something to check, once we sort this out."

They both scaled the wall, and, as Bojan went to jump down, Ryland grabbed his arm. "Look." One of the guards was in the tree but half off, and a steady drip of blood flowed to the ground.

"Shit," Bojan muttered, peering through the trees. "We've got a gunman at the pool with Leia. Bullard is there, and, of course, Lacy is right in the middle of it." He immediately sent her a message, telling her to be careful and that he was on the dividing wall.

Her voice slammed into his head. *I tried to get in and to help heal his mind, but it's broken. I can't get in.*

Don't try, he replied. *Some minds are just too cracked. If you get in there, it's easy to get lost, and I might not get you back out again.*

I'm trying to tweak the air around Leia to protect her—in case a bullet does come in her direction.

He paused at that and asked in wonder, *You can do that?*

I don't know, she muttered. *I'm trying. I'm trying anything. Somebody is about to get shot.*

I know that, Bojan snapped, *but better Bullard or me than you or Leia.*

I know, but …

At that, Ryland made his way through the tree to where his injured coworker was.

As Bojan watched the gunman, the branch made some creaking noises. The gunman shifted, but he didn't take his gaze off Bullard in front of him, obviously choosing who he considered to be the most dangerous person in front of him. Little did Charlie know that it was actually Lacy, but, as long as she didn't have to hurt somebody, she wouldn't. However, if it came down to that, he knew that Leia would win out.

Of course Leia will win out, Lacy snapped in his head, *but, as an energy worker and a healer, I can't take a life or hurt him in any way and expect to not have repercussions in my own work.*

Bojan knew that. Still, it wasn't a priority in his head right now. He knew for her it would be, but, for him, her life was paramount. He had twisted his energy for his own work, but it definitely hadn't become as much of his life as it had become in hers. And it was all understandable, but not Bojan's top priority at the moment. He watched as the tableau frozen in front of him played out, as the gunman roared at Bullard.

"It's your damn fault!"

"Yes," Bullard agreed. "Apparently it is. I'm willing to take full responsibility."

At that, the gunman just stared at him in shock. "Bring her back," he snapped. "You bring my sister back."

"I can't do that. She's dead."

"But this woman, … I shot her, and she's back. I killed her, and here she is alive again," Charlie roared. "So, if you can bring her back, you can bring my sister back."

Lacy shot Bullard an apologetic expression. "Sorry about that. I didn't know what to tell him."

Bullard stared at the broken man in front of him. "Even if I could bring her back, it's not something I can do in two seconds flat. You know that."

Charlie slowly nodded. "No, I guess it might take a little time," he muttered, sounding worried. He closed his eyes for a second and then looked down at Leia. "You go work on it now. I'll just keep her here with me."

"No, not a chance," Bullard declared, not giving an inch.

"Leia comes inside, where she is safe and away from you. Otherwise I won't do anything to help you."

At that, the gunman got furious again, and Lacy stepped forward. "You can keep me as a hostage instead," she suggested, as Bojan's voice slammed into her brain.

No!

The gunman looked at her suspiciously. "But I already killed you, and I can't kill you twice. You said so yourself."

Damn it, her own words were tripping her up now. "That's true," she admitted.

"You go in there with Bullard, and you bring her back. I want my sister back."

"What if we can't?" she asked. "Then what?"

"Then she dies," Charlie said, pointing his gun at Leia, followed by a shrug. "I don't care. It's an eye for an eye."

"But it's not an eye for an eye," Lacy argued with him, "because nobody did anything to your sister. The stroke killed her. It was just her time. I can't bring her back." Although, in the back of her mind, she was wondering if there was any way to contact her and maybe bring her into this conversation, so she could talk to her brother. Lacy knew that some people could talk to the dead, but Lacy had never been one of them.

She looked over at Leia, who had tears slowly forming in the corner of her eyes. This trauma, this acute stress was definitely not good for the mother or for her babies. Lacy noted the energy around the babies shifting, and that was not good either. Whether it was from the energy that she was pulling protectively around Leia or something else, Lacy didn't know. The last thing she wanted was something happening to the babies because of her own actions.

Lacy immediately stepped forward, walking at a firm

pace. "Leia will go inside now," she declared, her tone not giving Charlie any room to argue. "Absolutely no way will I agree to anything other than that."

As she reached for Leia, Lacy bent down and helped the pregnant woman to her feet, but the gunman tried to grab her. Lacy turned, and, instead of fighting him or shaking him off, she dropped backward, pulling his weight with her, and tumbled into the pool. Her hand was firmly around his, dragging him into the water. She heard Bullard dive into the water behind her. As she surfaced, Charlie was raising the gun up in the air to shoot.

In her mind, she pulled her energy tightly around Leia, while Lacy scrambled to the side of the pool. She heard voices and shouts, as everybody else came running. However, until that gun was secured, there would be nothing but panic for everyone. Then she heard gunfire—once, twice, three times. Silence fell afterward.

Bojan raced to the edge of the pool and, in one fell swoop, quickly helped Lacy out of the water. Then they both raced over to Leia, who was twisted on the lounger in agony. As Lacy neared her, she quickly released the protective energy.

Leia took in a deep breath. "I don't know why, but the pain is less now, and suddenly I can breathe easier."

Lacy winced. "Here. Let's get you up and inside. Then I want you lying down." The two of them helped a shaking Leia to her feet. Lacy cast a quick glance to the pool and realized that the gunman was floating on the water, as Bullard dragged his body closer to the edge. Ryland and several other men, including Pia, jumped in to subdue the shooter, if needed. Lacy had no idea where the bullets had gone, and she didn't care, as long as Leia didn't take any of them.

Bullard, looking frantic, called out, "Leia, are you okay?"

She lifted a hand and muttered, "I'll go lie down."

Lacy called back, "Bullard, we need you."

And, with that, dripping wet and shaky, Bullard and Lacy moved Leia into the surgery room and onto one of the beds.

Leia relaxed back on the bed and released a big breath. "I've never been so scared in my life," she whispered, tears pouring down her face.

Lacy wrapped her up in a big hug, even though she was soaking wet. "I'm so sorry, but that cramping you felt was me," she admitted.

Leia frowned at her in surprise. "What do you mean, the *cramping*? I thought I was shot." She moved her hands all over her belly. "He fired directly at me. I could practically see the bullet heading for my stomach, but there's no blood. I thought for sure I was shot."

"Yeah." Lacy took a deep breath herself, realizing that her energy application had worked. She sat on the edge of the bed and took a long shaky breath, suddenly feeling cold and afraid. "That was me too."

Bojan looked at her, and so did Leia. "You want to explain that?" Bojan asked.

"I pulled my energy in around you really tight. I was trying to make a deflective surface, that any bullet could bounce off of," she said, trying to explain the unexplainable. "Bullets are energy too, and I thought, if I could keep the energy vibrating at a fast-enough speed while wrapped around you, it should deflect the bullet. I was struggling to keep the energy shield up the whole time. When I went into the pool, I gave it an extra tug—in case Charlie managed to get away from me before anybody else could stop him. So, I need to look at you to be sure, but I presume the bullet bounced off you and has probably bruised you, but hopefully it didn't do any more damage. Just lie back while I have a look."

And, with Bojan standing at Leia's head and Bullard racing in behind, Lacy did a quick check and saw one hell of a bruise. She had no idea if the babies would be impacted in any way but hopefully not.

"There is a big bruise, and it may get bigger soon, although I can do something to mitigate that. The bullet didn't penetrate, but I can't be certain that there wasn't some damage."

Leia looked at her. "You mean from the impact?" she whispered.

Lacy nodded. "Yes, it's red, but it's not horrific."

At that, Leia burst into tears and then started to cramp up and cry, her body twisting. "Oh my God," she cried out, "the pain."

"Yeah, seems that whole scenario may have put you into labor," Lacy muttered.

"It's too early," Leia gasped.

"Definitely not as late as we would prefer, but it is what it is, and we're equipped and are prepared to deal with whatever comes our way."

Leia stared at Lacy, then looked over at the men, and they all nodded. Leia added, "It would be better for the twins to wait, even just another week or two."

Lacy agreed. "It would be better if we didn't have assholes in the world too, but right now these babies seem determined to come early. I'm not sure whether the blood vessels were damaged from the impact or there's something else going on," Lacy added, "but I can tell you that we're heading into hard labor." And, with that, she turned to Bojan. "Bullard and I have got this," she said, dismissing him, but then quickly pulled his sleeve before he left. "Could you go grab me some dry clothes?"

With a nod, Bojan took off at top speed. Bullard wrapped Leia up in his arms, then looked over at Lacy. "Will you do this?"

"Of course," she replied, staring at him. "I'm surprised you don't want to."

"I'll be here, but I feel like I belong on this side, helping her."

Lacy smiled at him. "That's very true, but—"

"You're one of the most professional doctors I've ever had a chance to work with," he declared, with a sigh, "and now I know why. I just wish to hell we could train more like you."

"Me too," she replied. "Then I wouldn't feel quite so guilty about not being able to help everybody."

"Just help Leia," Bullard muttered, his voice thick.

"I hear you," she murmured, "and I'll do my very best." And, with that, she quickly prepped, waiting for the dry clothes, so she wouldn't be dripping all over the floor, which would create another hazard. By the time Bojan returned with clothing for both Lacy and Bullard, she stepped away, stripped out of her bathing suit, and quickly threw on her sundress, then pulled on a pair of scrub bottoms. When she came back, Bojan was busy putting towels down to dry the floor, and then Bullard stepped away to change, while Lacy brought over the trays and the ultrasound.

As soon as she had everything ready for the fetal monitor and the ultrasound, Bullard stepped around to her side, just as Lacy said, "Okay, let's see what we've got here."

With that, he took a look and swore. "Damn, the babies are in fetal distress. I don't see any injury, and there definitely seems to be two," he declared, with a note of satisfaction in his voice.

Leia looked up at him, fear in her eyes. "But maybe this is where we lose one."

"We won't think along those lines," he stated firmly. "We're hanging on to both of our babies." With that, he looked over at Bojan and Lacy, his face suddenly stern. "Right?"

"We'll do our best," they both replied, practically in unison.

"Just know—"

At that, Bojan cut him off. "*No.* We will do everything we can, and this time it has to be enough."

Lacy looked up at Bojan to see the expression on his face, knowing how hard this had to be for him, but it wasn't the time to address it.

For the next hour, things got stressful, as Leia hit hard labor, the babies hell-bent on coming early. She was already past the point of getting an epidural, as the first baby crowned and presented itself. Lacy helped bring Leia and Bullard's son into the world. She handed the baby to his mother, resting him against her breast, while they fought for number two.

Bullard was at Lacy's side, wanting to get in there but also not wanting to, just in case he interrupted what she was doing. She reached out with her mind. *Bojan, I need help.* When he stepped forward, she said out loud, "Stay where you are, but I need your energy."

"Okay. How can I help?"

"Just like I twisted energy outside, ... I'll have to do some fancy maneuvering. He's smaller, and he will come out easier, but the cord is wrapped around his neck, and he's weak."

"You can use my energy any way you need to," Bojan offered.

She looked up at the ceiling, then smiled. "Thank you."

"I trust you, Lacy," he murmured.

Something about hearing those words made her stand taller somehow. She smiled broadly. "Thank you for that."

Very quickly, she needed more than two hands, as baby number two was suddenly here but very weak and not breathing. What she needed to do was something medical science could not offer, so she closed her eyes, as she pleaded for the spirit of this little guy to be strong enough to fight through the effects of everything that they'd already done, knowing so much more remained ahead for him.

When she heard the tiniest cry, she looked down, his arms and legs were moving ever-so-slightly, as he tried to breathe. When Bullard took him from her, Lacy tended to Leia. Bullard focused on clearing the second twin's airways, bringing him fully around. By the time he laid son number two into her arms, Leia had tears pouring down her face.

"And now you have twin sons," Bullard whispered in awe.

"No," she whispered, "*we* have twin sons."

Bullard smiled, and Lacy saw tears on his face as well. She sat down on the hard floor for a good minute to collect herself. Leia and Bullard were totally absorbed in the babies, when she finally looked up. She rose, walked over to the sanitization area, and washed up, then returned to the happy family, asking Bullard, "So you want to finish this off?"

Bullard looked over at Leia, who smiled, with a nod at Lacy. Bullard replied, "No, you can do it. The afterbirth will be along in a few minutes, and you've done great so far."

Turning to Bojan with a smile, Lacy said to Bojan, "You're off the hook. We're doing fine."

"Are you sure?" he asked.

She looked up at him, one eyebrow raised.

He shrugged, and, in her mind, he added, *Seems something's off.*

Without warning, blood poured from Leia down the table onto the floor.

Looking back at him, she turned to her patients, then jumped into action, as she realized Leia had started to hemorrhage. With both Bullard and Lacy working hard, they did everything they could to save her, as she laid here, now unconscious. Bojan snatched up both babies before they fell from her arms, then turned to look at Lacy helplessly.

In her head she called out to him. *Just give me your heart. Give me whatever love and energy you have.*

Then she quickly wrapped Leia up in as much energy as she could, using energy from Terkel and Clary and Clara and all the other healers she'd ever met, as she worked to stabilize Leia. They managed to stop the bleeding, but she'd lost a lot of blood. "Bullard, we will need a transfusion."

In a haze, he nodded. "You watch her. I'll get it going." Moving efficiently, he gathered what he needed and soon had the transfusion started. Minutes later, the monitors slowly reflected Leia's heart returning to a normal rhythm.

"Looks like we caught it," Bullard muttered.

She reached up a hand and pounded her palm against her forehead. "It was the impact of that damn bullet."

Bullard nodded. "That very well may be what did it, but

absolutely no way Leia or the babies would have survived the bullet. We have two sons and are so blessed. I just need her to stay alive."

Lacy asked Bojan to stick around, just in case. He nodded his agreement.

It took another twenty minutes before Leia murmured something and opened her eyes. She looked up at Bullard and whispered, "What happened?"

"You started to hemorrhage."

Lacy explained, "You ruptured on the inside, but you're fine now."

"You're not to move though," Bullard ordered. "We've got you hooked up to IVs, and we're getting some blood back into you. The babies are doing fine. I'll bring them over." With that, he pushed two nearby incubators closer.

Her eyes widened at the sight of the incubators. "Are they okay?" she gasped.

"They are, but things became dicey with you, so I figured they could use a little extra support," Bullard shared, as he reached for one of his sons and tucked him into her arms.

She stared down at the little boy in awe. "He's so beautiful," she whispered, looking up at Bullard.

"He is, and everything we ever wanted."

At that, she stared over at the second baby, still in the incubator. "He will be okay, right?" The fear had made her voice weak.

"He looks fine," Bullard confirmed. "He's stronger than he was, starting to fight a little harder."

"He needs a few days, since it was a rougher birth than we had hoped," Lacy murmured.

"But we made it," Leia said.

"We did, and we owe that to Lacy," Bullard noted, shaking his head. "I'm not even sure what all happened, but, by rights, … there is no way … If she … If Lacy hadn't been here, … we couldn't …" Bullard stopped, visibly choking up. "We couldn't have stopped the bleeding."

Leia looked up at him, her gaze steady. "But Lacy stopped it?"

"With Bullard's and Bojan's help," Lacy added.

Bullard nodded. "I don't know how. I don't even know what she or Bojan did, but I sure wish I could do it myself. I don't have the slightest idea of what just happened." Then they looked over at Lacy and Bojan.

"The good news is that the two of you were here for us, and, for that, you will always have our gratitude," Leia murmured.

Bullard nodded and smiled, leaning over to kiss his wife.

"Two babies, and both babies are fine. I love you all so very much."

CHAPTER 11

LACY HEADED TO bed that night, exhausted, yet feeling accomplished. The house buzzed with jubilation, celebration, and a quiet peacefulness, as everybody realized the crises were over now. Although it was dicey for a time—with the gunman and with the twin births and Leia's hemorrhage—everything was fine now, and the prevailing sentiment was gratitude.

As Lacy slipped away, after a final round of thanks from everyone, she lifted a hand. "Good night, all. I'm done in and heading to bed."

She headed up to her room and took a quick shower. When she walked out, Bojan was sitting on her bed.

He looked up at her and smiled. "You did good. Really good."

"No, *we* did good. I really pulled on your energy for that."

He nodded, as he stood and walked over, taking her into his arms. "And you did it. I was petrified it would be the same result all over again."

"I was too," she admitted, "but we must have done better this time."

"No, it's not a case of better," he disagreed, tucking her in close, his chin resting on the top of her head. "I think it's more than that. Maybe sometimes there is a final answer that we can't change," he admitted.

"Hey, for a while there, I was trying to figure out a way to make Charlie's dead sister appear so he could talk to her, but I just couldn't come up with a way to make that happen." Laughter rumbled up through his chest against her ear, making her smile. She leaned back to look up at him and stated, "I'm serious."

"I know you are," he noted, still grinning, "and it just makes me shake my head because it would never have occurred to me."

"No, you were probably ready to shoot him."

"Yeah, I absolutely was ready to shoot him," he declared. "That's the kind of work I do. You know the saying, … shoot first and ask questions later."

"Hardly," she replied, giving him a light slap on the chest. "You guys do a ton of work ahead of time."

"Yes, we do, but, when it comes down to those we love, we will err on the side of saving them."

"Well, in this case, we managed to save them all. But, man, I'm tired."

"Yeah, we did, and you best get to bed." He let his arms fall away, then turned and pulled back the sheet. "Your bed awaits."

She yawned as she sat down, then collapsed backward. "I am so done," she murmured.

"Of course you are. I'll talk to you in the morning."

"Or else you could stay," she whispered.

He froze, then turned to look back at her. "You know I want to, of course, but you're exhausted."

"I am, but I'll be exhausted whether you're here with me or not," she murmured, "and it would be really nice to wake up with you."

He smiled, as he came back over to sit down beside her. "Wake up with me?"

"Well, anything else is probably off the table at the moment. I couldn't stay awake no matter how good you are."

At that, he burst out laughing. "Go to sleep, and we'll see how you feel in the morning."

With that, she drifted off, yet she hadn't been asleep very long, when it seemed like her body began to pulse with a fire from deep within. She moaned, as she rolled over and then back again, not sure if she was caught in a nightmare or a dream. Then his voice whispered through her mind.

Take it easy. It's all right. Just relax.

She opened her eyes and whispered, "What's going on?"

"You were crying out in a nightmare, so I thought I would come up with an interesting way of getting you through it."

Then she realized that the sheet was off, and he had oil on his hands and was gently massaging her body. As his hands roamed up and down once again, she cried out in joy, as he slowly worked the muscles from her neck and shoulders, all the way down to her toes. His touch soothing her muscles was amazing, but when his thumbs flipped across her nipples, she cried out as passion surged within. "Dear God," she muttered, "a massage like that is pure luxury."

"Doesn't have to be," he murmured, "but it comes along with caring for somebody."

"That is something I haven't had a whole lot of experience with."

"And, for that, I'm sorry," he whispered. "I know it's because of me, and I promise to make it up to you."

She opened her eyes and stared at him in the darkness. "As much as a part of me says you don't have to, another part of me disagrees completely. So, yes, you should, especially this way."

He soothed her skin again, his palms creating magic with every stroke up and down her body. By the time he spread her thighs, she realized he was completely nude, and she welcomed him into her body, crying out with pleasure when he finally slipped deep inside. "That's where you belong."

"I know." He nuzzled her cheek and her nose and her chin. "And again, I'm so sorry."

She shook her head, then wrapped her arms around him. "I'm just glad we're here now," she murmured. "The waiting seemed to last forever."

He kissed her and then started to pulse his hips, his tongue sliding deep into her mouth, then pulling back as his body pulled back.

She shuddered in his arms and cried out, "Don't toy with me … please." Then he slammed deep inside her, once, twice, three times, until she couldn't even think and came apart in his arms. Only as she slowly came back did she hear him cry out above her, as he drove home, and she came apart a second time.

When she could finally think again, he whispered, "Don't worry. Go back to sleep now. Everything is okay."

"Are you sure?" she whispered.

"I'm sure, and you'll be fine. Go to sleep, and I'll make sure you're safe."

And, with that, she closed her eyes, but woke several more times in the night to similar treatments. By the time dawn crossed the horizon, she was exhausted, yet feeling more refreshed than ever. "You're a hell of a tonic," she murmured in his arms.

"I don't know about a tonic," he replied, 'but I'm glad

you got some sleep."

"You're not glad at all. I lost count of how many times you woke me up."

"Me too," he admitted, with a chuckle. "How sore are you?"

She looked up at him in surprise, then opened her thighs wide. "Not enough to stop."

"Good," he whispered, as he slid right in. "If you don't mind, I'd like to pick up the pace a bit." And, with that, it was almost as if he had lost control. He drove into her at an exhilarating pace, then came apart in her arms, as she held him close. Just as his final spasm racked through his system, her body climaxed once again in response. Then together, the two of them collapsed into a deep sleep.

EPILOGUE

BOJAN SMILED AT the group and announced, "We'll probably be back and forth. I really have no idea how this will work."

Bullard shrugged. "Well, as you've already seen, we have lots of people going back and forth with some regularity, so it's really fine with us. Any time you want to come, it's all good, and we'll be happy to have you."

Lacy walked over to where Leia held the twins, now six weeks old. Lacy kissed all three of them. "You look after these two, *huh*? Just remember to put them down once in a while," she teased, with a grin. "It's good for all of you."

"Oh, stop. I'm not that bad." Leia looked up at her friend with a huge smile. "You have no idea how grateful I am."

"Your face tells me every day," Lacy declared, as she crouched in front of them. "We'll be back, and, in a couple years, we'll come again to repeat the process."

At that future mention, his shock clearly evident on his facial expression, Bullard stammered, "Wait, what?"

Leia looked at Lacy in delight. "Seriously?"

Lacy nodded, then leaned forward and whispered, "Girls next time." She stepped back and winked at Leia, then gave Bullard a big hug. "We're off to Terkel's place because chaos is about to begin over there."

"Well, it's bound to happen," Bullard noted, "but no babies yet, right?"

"Not yet, but it won't be long, and I'm hoping to get some training in. Although Terkel says I should be training some people over there, but that's hardly the case."

Bullard nodded. "Whatever Terkel's got planned, you go for it. We're just glad to have you as part of the family."

And, with Bojan and Lacy holding hands, the two of them said goodbye to the rest of the group.

As they headed to the airport, where Bullard's plane was waiting to take them to England, Lacy looked up at Bojan. "Kind of amazing that we have this much family all over the place."

"I know," Bojan agreed. "Are you okay to go to Terkel's place?"

"We need to," she said, "and it's probably really where we belong, but we should definitely come back and forth."

"Absolutely."

They boarded the plane and waited for the pilot to say they were ready to take off.

Bojan's phone rang. "Hello, Terkel. … Yeah, we're on the plane right now, just waiting to take off. … Okay. Sure, that's not a problem. The more the merrier, as they say. Who is it?"

Just then, somebody bolted onto the plane, then looked up at Bojan and smiled. "Made it."

Bojan laughed and told Terk, "It's all good. Riff's here."

She looked over at Riff. "I saw you at the dividing wall, when the shooting was going on."

He grinned. "Yeah, you sure did. Two of those shots were mine, taking out the gunman," he shared. "I tend to be there, but not there, … kind of turning up in odd places, wherever I'm needed."

She frowned at him. "Does Bullard know?"

"He does, but now I'm heading back because Terkel apparently has another case."

"Well, I hope it doesn't involve me," Bojan added. "I need a little downtime."

"Oh, that's all right. He's hoping to use you for security at home," Riff shared. "It's for someone else."

At that, Terkel's voice came through loud and clear to all three of them. *Bojan, it's about an old friend of yours. Langdon Morrissey is his name.*

Yeah, I know him, but why?

He put out a call looking for you because you told him if he ever ran into trouble to give you a call. And, if not you, then me. So, I ended up getting the call because you were out of commission.

Right, so what does he want?

Something about his mother being murdered and her caregiver being kidnapped.

At that, Bojan frowned. *Seriously?*

Yeah, but I don't know much about this guy.

Langdon is awesome, but she's not actually his mother.

Terkel replied, *I got that.*

She's one of the cabinet ministers, Bojan added. *He talks about her as being his mother, but it's not in a biological sense. He was one of those extra kids who came home one day and stayed. But the caregiver, now that's interesting. I thought her caregiver was Molly.*

That's the name I have. Apparently Molly's been kidnapped.

Ah, hell. This shit just never ends.

I'm sending Riff over as backup. Langdon already has some

leads, but he doesn't want to go into this blind, and he understands that we have some skills, Terk shared, with a laugh.

Yeah, that's because he has skills himself, Bojan noted. *So, if he's looking for backup, he's expecting it to get ugly. I can go,* he offered, looking over at Lacy.

No, if we need you, we'll call you, Terkel replied, sounding adamant. *Bullard is also sending over Eton, who will be there to help out. However, if this Langdon guy's got skills, I'd like to know what kind of skills we're talking about.*

Yeah, you and me both. He's never really talked to me about it. I just know they exist.

Seems to be the right time to find out.

I'm wondering why Langdon hasn't gone after Molly, Riff noted, with a frown.

Bojan looked up at him and nodded. *Good question, and they used to be an item, by the way. But I also know that Langdon was heading in for surgery. He's missing a leg but had a couple ribs rebuilt in order to protect his lungs. That was the last I heard, but I don't know what happened after that.*

Maybe his health is stopping him from rescuing Molly then, as something is off if he asked for help.

Absolutely. He's always been a loner but a can-do type of guy. And he would never ask for help.

Well, this time he did, Terk murmured. *And help he'll get.*

Bojan nodded. *That makes sense because Molly was his heart.*

And he'll get all the help he needs, Terk declared.

This concludes Book 3 of Terk's Guardians: Bojan.
Read about Langdon: Terk's Guardians, Book 4

Terk's Guardians: Langdon
(Book #4)

Langdon hasn't been in a good place for a long time, but it was time enough to chase away the woman he'd loved since forever. Unable to reach her to make it right, he realizes she's disappeared—and not by choice. He then finds out why Molly was kidnapped and by whom.

Molly would do just about anything for Langdon, yet being used as leverage to force him to act wasn't part of the plan. But escaping would take more than her special energy skills, abilities her captors are unaware of. She needs to keep it that way.

Now if only she could open the psychic door she'd slammed shut between her and Langdon to let him know what was happening—before he was forced to do something that could kill them both …

Find Book 4 here!
To find out more visit Dale Mayer's website.
https://geni.us/DMSLangdon

Author's Note

Thank you for reading Bojan: Terk's Guardians, Book 3! If you enjoyed the book, please take a moment and leave a short review.

Dear reader,

I love to hear from readers, and you can contact me at my website: www.dalemayer.com or at my Facebook author page. To be informed of new releases and special offers, sign up for my newsletter or follow me on BookBub. And if you are interested in joining Dale Mayer's Reader Group, here is the Facebook sign up page.
http://geni.us/DaleMayerFBGroup

Cheers,
Dale Mayer

About the Author

Dale Mayer is a *USA Today* best-selling author, best known for her SEALs military romances, her Psychic Visions series, and her Lovely Lethal Garden cozy series. Her contemporary romances are raw and full of passion and emotion (Broken But … Mending, Hathaway House series). Her thrillers will keep you guessing (Kate Morgan, By Death series), and her romantic comedies will keep you giggling (*It's a Dog's Life*, a stand-alone novella; and the Broken Protocols series, starring Charming Marvin, the cat).

Dale honors the stories that come to her—and some of them are crazy, break all the rules and cross multiple genres!

To go with her fiction, she also writes nonfiction in many different fields, with books available on résumé writing, companion gardening, and the US mortgage system. All her books are available in print and ebook format.

Connect with Dale Mayer Online

Dale's Website – www.dalemayer.com
Twitter – @DaleMayer
Facebook Page – geni.us/DaleMayerFBFanPage
Facebook Group – geni.us/DaleMayerFBGroup
BookBub – geni.us/DaleMayerBookbub
Instagram – geni.us/DaleMayerInstagram
Goodreads – geni.us/DaleMayerGoodreads
Newsletter – geni.us/DaleNews

Also by Dale Mayer

Published Adult Books:

Shadow Recon
Magnus, Book 1
Rogan, Book 2
Egan, Book 3
Barret, Book 4
Whalen, Book 5
Nikolai, Book 6

Bullard's Battle
Ryland's Reach, Book 1
Cain's Cross, Book 2
Eton's Escape, Book 3
Garret's Gambit, Book 4
Kano's Keep, Book 5
Fallon's Flaw, Book 6
Quinn's Quest, Book 7
Bullard's Beauty, Book 8
Bullard's Best, Book 9
Bullard's Battle, Books 1–2
Bullard's Battle, Books 3–4
Bullard's Battle, Books 5–6
Bullard's Battle, Books 7–8

Terkel's Team

Damon's Deal, Book 1
Wade's War, Book 2
Gage's Goal, Book 3
Calum's Contact, Book 4
Rick's Road, Book 5
Scott's Summit, Book 6
Brody's Beast, Book 7
Terkel's Twist, Book 8
Terkel's Triumph, Book 9

Terk's Guardians

Radar, Book 1
Legend, Book 2
Bojan, Book 3
Langdon, Book 4

Kate Morgan

Simon Says… Hide, Book 1
Simon Says… Jump, Book 2
Simon Says… Ride, Book 3
Simon Says… Scream, Book 4
Simon Says… Run, Book 5
Simon Says… Walk, Book 6
Simon Says… Forgive, Book 7
Simon Says… Swim, Book 8

Hathaway House

Aaron, Book 1
Brock, Book 2
Cole, Book 3
Denton, Book 4

The K9 Files

Rowan, Book 10

Caleb, Book 11

Kurt, Book 12

Tucker, Book 13

Harley, Book 14

Kyron, Book 15

Jenner, Book 16

Rhys, Book 17

Landon, Book 18

Harper, Book 19

Kascius, Book 20

Declan, Book 21

Bauer, Book 22

The K9 Files, Books 1–2

The K9 Files, Books 3–4

The K9 Files, Books 5–6

The K9 Files, Books 7–8

The K9 Files, Books 9–10

The K9 Files, Books 11–12

Lovely Lethal Gardens

Arsenic in the Azaleas, Book 1

Bones in the Begonias, Book 2

Corpse in the Carnations, Book 3

Daggers in the Dahlias, Book 4

Evidence in the Echinacea, Book 5

Footprints in the Ferns, Book 6

Gun in the Gardenias, Book 7

Handcuffs in the Heather, Book 8

Ice Pick in the Ivy, Book 9

Jewels in the Juniper, Book 10

Killer in the Kiwis, Book 11

Psychic Visions Series

Unmasked

Deep Beneath

From the Ashes

Stroke of Death

Ice Maiden

Snap, Crackle…

What If…

Talking Bones

String of Tears

Inked Forever

Insanity

Psychic Visions Books 1–3

Psychic Visions Books 4–6

Psychic Visions Books 7–9

By Death Series

Touched by Death

Haunted by Death

Chilled by Death

By Death Books 1–3

Broken Protocols – Romantic Comedy Series

Cat's Meow

Cat's Pajamas

Cat's Cradle

Cat's Claus

Broken Protocols 1-4

Broken and… Mending

Skin

Scars

Scales (of Justice)

Broken but... Mending 1-3

Glory
Genesis
Tori
Celeste
Glory Trilogy

Biker Blues
Morgan: Biker Blues, Volume 1
Cash: Biker Blues, Volume 2

SEALs of Honor
Mason: SEALs of Honor, Book 1
Hawk: SEALs of Honor, Book 2
Dane: SEALs of Honor, Book 3
Swede: SEALs of Honor, Book 4
Shadow: SEALs of Honor, Book 5
Cooper: SEALs of Honor, Book 6
Markus: SEALs of Honor, Book 7
Evan: SEALs of Honor, Book 8
Mason's Wish: SEALs of Honor, Book 9
Chase: SEALs of Honor, Book 10
Brett: SEALs of Honor, Book 11
Devlin: SEALs of Honor, Book 12
Easton: SEALs of Honor, Book 13
Ryder: SEALs of Honor, Book 14
Macklin: SEALs of Honor, Book 15
Corey: SEALs of Honor, Book 16
Warrick: SEALs of Honor, Book 17
Tanner: SEALs of Honor, Book 18
Jackson: SEALs of Honor, Book 19

Kanen: SEALs of Honor, Book 20

Nelson: SEALs of Honor, Book 21

Taylor: SEALs of Honor, Book 22

Colton: SEALs of Honor, Book 23

Troy: SEALs of Honor, Book 24

Axel: SEALs of Honor, Book 25

Baylor: SEALs of Honor, Book 26

Hudson: SEALs of Honor, Book 27

Lachlan: SEALs of Honor, Book 28

Paxton: SEALs of Honor, Book 29

Bronson: SEALs of Honor, Book 30

Hale: SEALs of Honor, Book 31

SEALs of Honor, Books 1–3

SEALs of Honor, Books 4–6

SEALs of Honor, Books 7–10

SEALs of Honor, Books 11–13

SEALs of Honor, Books 14–16

SEALs of Honor, Books 17–19

SEALs of Honor, Books 20–22

SEALs of Honor, Books 23–25

Heroes for Hire

Levi's Legend: Heroes for Hire, Book 1

Stone's Surrender: Heroes for Hire, Book 2

Merk's Mistake: Heroes for Hire, Book 3

Rhodes's Reward: Heroes for Hire, Book 4

Flynn's Firecracker: Heroes for Hire, Book 5

Logan's Light: Heroes for Hire, Book 6

Harrison's Heart: Heroes for Hire, Book 7

Saul's Sweetheart: Heroes for Hire, Book 8

Dakota's Delight: Heroes for Hire, Book 9

Tyson's Treasure: Heroes for Hire, Book 10

Jace's Jewel: Heroes for Hire, Book 11
Rory's Rose: Heroes for Hire, Book 12
Brandon's Bliss: Heroes for Hire, Book 13
Liam's Lily: Heroes for Hire, Book 14
North's Nikki: Heroes for Hire, Book 15
Anders's Angel: Heroes for Hire, Book 16
Reyes's Raina: Heroes for Hire, Book 17
Dezi's Diamond: Heroes for Hire, Book 18
Vince's Vixen: Heroes for Hire, Book 19
Ice's Icing: Heroes for Hire, Book 20
Johan's Joy: Heroes for Hire, Book 21
Galen's Gemma: Heroes for Hire, Book 22
Zack's Zest: Heroes for Hire, Book 23
Bonaparte's Belle: Heroes for Hire, Book 24
Noah's Nemesis: Heroes for Hire, Book 25
Tomas's Trials: Heroes for Hire, Book 26
Carson's Choice: Heroes for Hire, Book 27
Dante's Decision: Heroes for Hire, Book 28
Steven's Solace: Heroes for Hire, Book 29
Heroes for Hire, Books 1–3
Heroes for Hire, Books 4–6
Heroes for Hire, Books 7–9
Heroes for Hire, Books 10–12
Heroes for Hire, Books 13–15
Heroes for Hire, Books 16–18
Heroes for Hire, Books 19–21
Heroes for Hire, Books 22–24

SEALs of Steel

Badger: SEALs of Steel, Book 1
Erick: SEALs of Steel, Book 2
Cade: SEALs of Steel, Book 3

Talon: SEALs of Steel, Book 4
Laszlo: SEALs of Steel, Book 5
Geir: SEALs of Steel, Book 6
Jager: SEALs of Steel, Book 7
The Final Reveal: SEALs of Steel, Book 8
SEALs of Steel, Books 1–4
SEALs of Steel, Books 5–8
SEALs of Steel, Books 1–8

The Mavericks

Kerrick, Book 1
Griffin, Book 2
Jax, Book 3
Beau, Book 4
Asher, Book 5
Ryker, Book 6
Miles, Book 7
Nico, Book 8
Keane, Book 9
Lennox, Book 10
Gavin, Book 11
Shane, Book 12
Diesel, Book 13
Jerricho, Book 14
Killian, Book 15
Hatch, Book 16
Corbin, Book 17
Aiden, Book 18
The Mavericks, Books 1–2
The Mavericks, Books 3–4
The Mavericks, Books 5–6
The Mavericks, Books 7–8

The Mavericks, Books 9–10
The Mavericks, Books 11–12

Standalone Novellas
It's a Dog's Life
Riana's Revenge
Second Chances

Published Young Adult Books:

Family Blood Ties Series
Vampire in Denial
Vampire in Distress
Vampire in Design
Vampire in Deceit
Vampire in Defiance
Vampire in Conflict
Vampire in Chaos
Vampire in Crisis
Vampire in Control
Vampire in Charge
Family Blood Ties Set 1–3
Family Blood Ties Set 1–5
Family Blood Ties Set 4–6
Family Blood Ties Set 7–9
Sian's Solution, A Family Blood Ties Series Prequel
  Novelette

Design series
Dangerous Designs
Deadly Designs
Darkest Designs

Design Series Trilogy

Standalone

In Cassie's Corner
Gem Stone (a Gemma Stone Mystery)
Time Thieves

Published Non-Fiction Books:

Career Essentials

Career Essentials: The Résumé
Career Essentials: The Cover Letter
Career Essentials: The Interview
Career Essentials: 3 in 1

www.ingramcontent.com/pod-product-compliance
Lightning Source LLC
Chambersburg PA
CBHW070338200726
48294CB00003B/698